"What do you want for yourself?" Myles asked.

Zabrina said the first thing that came to mind. "Sex."

Myles lowered his head, unable to believe what he'd just heard. "You're kidding, aren't you?"

"Do I look like I'm kidding?"

Surprised by her admission, Myles stared at her in disbelief.

"Why are you looking at me like that? Would it be less shocking if the roles were reversed, and you were the one saying that you wanted to have sex with me?"

"Is that what you want from me?" he asked, recovering his composure.

"Sure, but only if you're up for it," she countered with a smile. "It would just be for the summer."

Books by Rochelle Alers

Kimani Romance

Bittersweet Love
Sweet Deception

Silhouette Desire

A Younger Man
*The Long Hot Summer
*Very Private Duty
*Beyond Business

*The Blackstones of Virginia

ROCHELLE ALERS

has been hailed by readers and booksellers alike as one of today's most popular African-American authors of women's fiction. With nearly two million copies of her novels in print, Ms. Alers is a regular on the Waldenbooks, Borders and *Essence* bestseller lists, and has been the recipient of numerous awards, including the Gold Pen Award, the Emma Award, the Vivian Stephens Award for Excellence in Romance Writing, the *RT Book Reviews* Career Achievement Award and the Zora Neale Hurston Literary Award. A native New Yorker, Ms. Alers currently lives on Long Island. Visit her Web site at: www.rochellealers.com.

Sweet Deception

ROCHELLE ALERS

KIMANI
ROMANCE

Blessed are the meek: for they shall inherit the earth.
—*Matthew 5:5*

KIMANI PRESS™

ISBN-13: 978-0-373-86140-8

Recycling programs
for this product may
not exist in your area.

SWEET DECEPTION

www.kimanipress.com

Printed in U.S.A.

Dear Reader,

How many times have you wished for a second chance with someone you loved then lost?

Zabrina Cooper's wish is granted when she reunites with Myles Eaton at his sister's wedding. But will the secrets she has coveted for more than a decade bring them closer—or destroy a future that promises forever?

In the second installment of the Eaton family miniseries, I continue the theme of second-chance love. However, unlike Belinda and Griffin Rice, Myles only has the summer to uncover why—just two weeks before the wedding!—Zabrina ended their engagement to marry an influential Philadelphia politician. As you read *Sweet Deception*, please keep in mind what Zabrina has had to sacrifice in order to protect her family.

Look for Chandra Eaton's *Sweet Dreams* early 2010 when the former peace corps teacher misplaces journals filled with her erotic dreams.

Visit my Web site at www.rochellealers.com.

Rochelle

Chapter 1

The buzz of the intercom echoed throughout the spacious co-op. "I'll get it," Myles Eaton announced loudly from the bedroom. Pressing the button on the intercom, he spoke into the speaker. "Yes?"

"Mr. Eaton, there's a take-out delivery in the lobby for you."

"Please send it up."

Zabrina Mixon stepped inside the apartment from the terrace, closing the sliding-glass door behind her. She liked seeing her fiancé dressed casually in T-shirts, shorts and sandals rather than a business suit. Suits always made him appear staid, standoffish. Her gaze lingered on his muscular calves before moving up to his broad chest and finally his ruggedly handsome face. His face was symmetrical with a dark brown complexion, deep-set eyes and a lean, angular jaw that became more pronounced whenever he smiled. His gorgeous smile drew attention to his perfectly aligned white teeth.

She couldn't remember when she hadn't been in love with Myles Eaton. He'd taught her to ride a bike, and whenever she fell he'd brushed off the dirt from her scraped knees and elbows, then helped her to get back on. Her infatuation began in childhood when Myles became her prince.

"I've finished setting the table," said Zabrina.

Myles smiled at his fiancée. He hadn't believed his luck when he'd finally opened his eyes to his sister's best friend. He'd thought of her as a younger sister until her eighteenth birthday. It was the first time that *he* had kissed her. A few years before that *she* had kissed him before he left Philadelphia to attend Penn State. Her excuse was that she hadn't wanted him to miss her.

Zabrina kissing Myles had left him feeling unsettled, because at eighteen he was an adult—a sexually active adult, and he had not wanted to take advantage of a teenage girl. However, several years later, they both had changed. Zabrina left home to attend Vanderbilt University School of Nursing in Tennessee while he was headed to Pittsburgh to enroll in Duquesne University School of Law.

By the time she was in college, there was nothing prepubescent about Zabrina Mixon. She was no longer tall and gangly, her body had filled out with womanly curves and her voice had deepened to a low, sexy tone that never failed to send shivers up and down his body. The sound of her voice was only matched by the luminous hazel eyes that pulled him in and refused to let him go.

Zabrina had a way of seducing him without saying a word. All she had to do was look at him and he forgot any woman he'd ever known. They reconnected whenever they returned home during semester breaks, but it wasn't until she'd graduated from college that he'd proposed marriage and she'd accepted. They'd talked about having a June wedding, but the establishment where they wanted to have the reception was booked solid until October. They'd reserved the last Saturday in October, because neither wanted a winter wedding given the unpredictable weather.

Myles winked at Zabrina. "Go back outside and relax, baby. The food is on its way up and I'll bring everything out to the terrace."

She returned the wink, then retraced her steps. Settling into an oversize pillow on the terrace of Myles's fourteenth-floor co-op, Zabrina waited for him to join her.

After her twelve-hour shift at a busy Philadelphia municipal hospital, she'd checked her cell phone for messages earlier that day. There were two: one from her father to let her know he was having dinner with an up-and-coming local politician who wanted Isaac Mixon to run his campaign for reelection to the state assembly, and the second from Myles.

After listening to Myles's message asking her to meet him for dinner at his apartment, she'd gone home to shower and change her clothes, then walked the short distance from the condominium where she lived with her father to Myles's high-rise. The doorman at the luxury building had greeted her by name. Within days of Myles slipping the diamond engagement ring onto her finger, he'd given her a key to his co-op and had officially notified the building management to grant her complete access.

The sun slipped lower, taking with it the intense summer heat as a cool breeze swept over her face and body. Lighted votives that she'd positioned around the terrace flickered like fireflies with the encroaching darkness. Philadelphia had experienced the most brutal heat wave it'd had in years. A steady two-day rain had finally broken the ninety-plus-degree heat and the streets in the City of Brotherly Love once again teemed with residents and tourists taking advantage of the more comfortable summer temperatures.

Turning her gaze away from the panoramic view of the twin glass spires of Liberty Place soaring above the Philadelphia skyline, Zabrina saw Myles holding a shopping bag from which emanated the most mouthwatering aroma.

"Something smells wonderful."

Myles leaned over and kissed the hair she'd brushed off her face and secured in a single braid. "That must be my linguine with garlic and olive oil."

"Phew," Zabrina said, pinching her nostrils. "Remind me not to kiss you."

"What if I brush my teeth and use mouthwash?"

She wrinkled her nose. "I'll think about it," she teased.

Myles sat opposite Zabrina, reached into the bag and took out a small container of Caesar salad, then two larger containers with his entrée and Zabrina's Caesar salad with grilled chicken. "Wait, darling, we're missing something."

Zabrina examined the place settings. "What's missing?"

"Wine and music."

"What are we celebrating, Myles?"

He stood and leaned over the table. "My love for you, darling."

Zabrina rose to brush her mouth over his, her eyes filling with tears. She never tired of hearing him say that he loved her. "And I love you, too, Myles Adam Eaton."

Myles returned with a bottle of wine, glasses and a small portable radio that he'd tuned to an all-music station.

He filled the wineglasses with a light rosé, raising his goblet in a toast. "Here's to the sexiest and most beautiful woman in the world. I'm counting down the days until I can make you my wife."

Zabrina paused, trying to keep her fragile emotions under control. She touched her glass to his. "Here's to the man who makes me feel alive, look forward to tomorrow and to all my tomorrows as his wife."

A wave of sadness came over her like a rushing wave. She didn't know why, but she felt like crying. In exactly three months she would exchange vows with the man she loved beyond words. How many women, she wondered, were fortunate enough to marry the first man they'd fallen in love with? Not too many, so she'd counted herself blessed.

"Here, here," Myles intoned before taking a sip of wine.

"I hope your client is toasting you for keeping his butt out of prison."

A scowl settled across his features. He'd made it a practice not to discuss his work with Zabrina, but the name of his high-profile client was on the tongue of most Philadelphians after the aide to the mayor had been charged with a sex crime.

"Jack Tolliver was innocent and apparently the prosecutor agreed with me when he threw out the charges for lack of evidence."

"But didn't he admit to sleeping with the woman?"

Myles rolled his eyes upward. "Yes, baby."

"So, who's to say it was consensual?"

"He said he didn't rape her."

Zabrina gave him a quizzical look. "And you believed him?"

"Yes."

"Just because he said he didn't do it?" She gestured with her fork. "Darling, Jack Tolliver is a lying, cheating politician who wouldn't recognize the truth if it jumped up and bit him on the ass."

Myles angled his head. "Are you angry with Jack because he cheated on his wife with another woman, or are you angry because he's a politician?"

"It's because he's a politician, Myles. I know he's human, but when he stands up in front of millions of voters asking for their trust, the least he could do is not betray their trust—and his wife's—by creeping with a married woman."

"You're too young to be so jaded when it comes to politicians, baby. Perhaps you should stay away from your father's friends."

He'd gotten the judge to dismiss the case because the plaintiff's rape kit had turned up evidence that she'd slept with his client *and* with another man. If Myles was going to toast anything it was that DNA forensics had helped to exonerate or convict suspects in some of the most violent crimes.

"My father's friends are just that—his friends. The only interaction I have with them is when I stand in as his hostess. Other than that, I loathe their fake smiles, weak handshakes, lecherous stares and the rare occasion when they brush against me pretending that it was an accident."

Myles went completely still, his frown deepening. "Is someone bothering you?"

She waved a hand. "No, darling. Most of them are around the same age as my father, so I ignore them."

Zabrina stared at her fiancé across the small space. Lately, she and Myles saw less and less of each other. Her eight-hour shift rotated every three months, and then there was overtime. Myles had passed the bar and clerked for a judge before becoming a trial lawyer for a Philadelphia firm handling high-profile cases. His ultimate goal was to make partner within ten years.

Swallowing a mouthful of pasta, Myles met Zabrina's eyes. They appeared catlike in the candlelight. "Can you take a couple of days off?"

"Why?"

"I'd like for us to go away together so we can spend some quality time together."

Reaching over the table, Myles grasped her hands. "I saw more of you before we were engaged than I do now."

Zabrina sobered. He'd read her mind. "That's because *you've* become a workaholic."

"I want to make partner, Brina."

She wanted to tell Myles there were no guarantees that he would make partner even if he worked ninety hours a week, while winning every case for the firm. But she held her tongue because she didn't want him to think she wasn't supportive.

"Where do you want to go?" she asked.

His grip tightened on her fingers. "I'll leave that up to you."

It took only seconds for her to make a decision. "I want to go to Buenos Aires."

"Buenos Aires, Argentina?" She nodded. "What's in Buenos Aires?"

"Tango lessons," Zabrina replied. "I want our first dance as husband and wife to be a tango, and what better place to learn the dance of love and passion than in Argentina?"

Rising, Myles walked around the circular table and gently pulled Zabrina to her feet. He dipped his head and pressed his mouth to the column of her scented neck. "I happen to believe we dance very well together."

She giggled like a child. "Are you talking about the horizontal mambo?"

"Yes, I am."

Moving into his embrace, Zabrina wrapped her arms around Myles's waist. He felt so good, smelled so incredibly delicious. His cologne was specially blended to complement his body's natural pheromones. She closed her eyes and smiled. "I seem to have forgotten the steps."

Pulling her closer, Myles reveled in the soft crush of firm breasts against his chest. "How long has it been, baby?" he whispered.

Zabrina thought back to the last time they'd made love. "It's been at least three weeks."

"I promise to make love to…"

She placed her fingertips over his mouth, stopping his words. "Don't promise. Just do it."

Bending slightly, Myles swept his fiancée up into his arms and carried her off the terrace to the bedroom. He hadn't wanted to believe he hadn't made love to Zabrina in weeks. When, he thought, had his work taken precedence over the woman he loved and planned to marry? She'd become the most important thing in his life, yet he'd let something else replace her.

Their candlelit terrace dinner was forgotten when he placed Zabrina on the bed, his body following hers. It took less than a minute for Myles to remove her sandals, sundress and panties. The light from the bedside-table lamp, dimmed to its lowest setting, spilled over her nude body, making it appear like a statue of gold.

He undressed and then moved over her. "I can't believe

I've neglected you for so long. I want you to remind me when I get so caught up straightening out other people's lives that I forget what I have right in front of me."

Zabrina buried her face between Myles's neck and shoulder at the same time her arms went around his waist. "How often do you want me to remind you?"

"Every night," he said in her ear.

She opened her eyes and smiled. "If that's the case, then I'll be certain to do it."

Myles breathed a kiss under her ear, along the column of her neck and to her throat. His rapacious tongue charted a path down her body as he suckled one breast, then the other. Zabrina's breathing came faster and faster. His tongue swept over her like a wild cat savoring its kill. He tasted her belly. Effortlessly he turned her over to taste her back, nipping the skin covering her hips. Pressing a kiss to the small of her back, he moved lower to the area between her legs. Myles anchored his hands under her thighs and pulled her up into a kneeling position.

Zabrina was on fire! It was as if Myles had struck a match and set her ablaze. The increasing heat between her legs escalated as her hips undulated in a natural rhythm that communicated a long-denied need.

Myles felt and inhaled the rising desire from the slender body pushing back against his belly. He hardened quickly, so quickly he feared spilling his passion on the sheets. Guiding his erection, he eased it between Zabrina's thighs. The two of them sighed as flesh closed around flesh, making them one.

Grasping her waist with both hands, he held her captive as she pushed back to meet his strong thrusts. He closed his eyes and bit down on his lip to keep the groans building in his throat from escaping, but the rising passion was too much and he moaned as if in pain. But it was the most pleasurable pain he'd ever experienced.

He didn't know what it was about Zabrina Mixon, but once she had offered him her virginal body, every woman in his past had ceased to exist. And what he couldn't understand was how had he gone nearly a month without making love with her. Had his quest to make partner taken precedence over the woman he loved? Zabrina didn't want him to make promises, but he promised himself that tonight would signal change. He would put his fiancée first and his career second.

Heat began in Zabrina's core and spread outward like spokes on a wheel. Reaching for the top of the headboard, she held on to the carved mahogany as if it were a lifeline. And at that moment it was. Unfamiliar sensations raced through her body, cutting a swath of pleasure that lifted her beyond ecstasy. She was caught up in a maelstrom of passion that bordered on hysteria. Her throat was burning from the screams that emanated from somewhere she hadn't known existed, then, without warning, the orgasms came, one after the other, overlapping until she felt herself succumbing to the deepest desire she'd ever experienced.

Myles held Zabrina's waist in a punishing grip as he rested his head on her back. He clenched his teeth so tightly his jaw ached, and try as he could he couldn't hold back the passion threatening to erupt at any moment. Sucking in a lungful of breath, he surrendered to the raging fire in his loins, his body shaking like a stalwart tree in a storm.

In a moment of madness they'd surrendered all they were and would ever be to each other.

Chapter 2

The reason you've been feeling so tired is that you're pregnant.

The doctor's diagnosis played over and over in Zabrina Mixon's head until she felt as if it were a mantra. Warm tears spilled down her face, blurring her vision, but she could still see the indicator wand that came with the home pregnancy test. She *was* pregnant. She, a registered nurse, who hadn't believed her ob-gyn, had stopped at a local drugstore and bought a kit to conduct her own test.

Her gynecologist had changed her contraceptive three times, the third being a lower-dose pill. The other two had adverse side effects: headaches, nausea and tender breasts. Apparently the lowest dose was too low, because she was now among the one percent of women who'd gotten pregnant on the pill. She and Myles Eaton had talked about starting a family, but at twenty-three Zabrina had wanted to wait at least two years. Two years would give her time to adjust to married life.

She'd been counting the days before she would exchange vows with the man she'd fallen in love with after they'd only dated a month. He'd waited a year to propose marriage and she'd accepted. It was now two weeks before her wedding and she would walk down the aisle with a new life growing inside her. It wasn't how she'd planned to start married life.

Discarding the pregnancy kit in the wastebasket, Zabrina washed her hands. She walked out of the bathroom, stopping when she heard voices coming from the living room. She recognized her father's voice and another that was vaguely familiar. A third voice, this one deeper than the others stopped her mid-stride. This voice she knew. It belonged to Thomas Cooper, her father's protégé. Alarmed, she made her way into the living room.

"What's going on here?"

Isaac Mixon turned when he heard his daughter's voice. "When did you get home?"

Zabrina's gaze shifted from her father to the other two men. It was obvious they'd thought they were alone. "I got here about twenty minutes ago." She glared at City Council President Thomas Cooper, who, it was widely rumored, had aspirations to become Philadelphia's next mayor. "Were you threatening my father?"

Thomas Cooper flashed a smile, the one he'd perfected for the media and his constituents. "Zabrina, please come and sit down."

Zabrina's eyebrows lifted. "You're inviting me to sit down in *my* own home?"

The practiced smile vanished quickly. "Mixon, I think

you'd better convince your daughter to listen to what we have to tell her, or she'll read about your arrest in tomorrow's Philly *Inquirer.*"

Isaac crossed the room and cradled his daughter to his chest. "Please, Brina, let me handle this."

Light brown eyes flecked with hints of green studied the face of the man who'd protected her since her mother had died the year Zabrina had celebrated her seventh birthday. Isaac Mixon had become father *and* mother, refusing to remarry because he claimed he didn't want to subject her to a dreadful stepmother. She knew he dated women, but he'd never brought one home.

She nodded. "Okay, Daddy." Isaac pulled out a straight-back chair for Zabrina to sit in, and she watched as her father walked over to the floor-to-ceiling windows to peer out at the Philadelphia skyline.

It was the third man in the room who spoke first. "Miss Mixon, your father has been misappropriating monies from Councilman Cooper's campaign contributions."

A heavy silence filled the room as four pairs of eyes exchanged glances, and Zabrina wondered how many more shocks she would have to endure in one day. First there was the news that she was carrying a child, and now the threat that her father was facing arrest for stealing money from the man whose political career he'd shepherded from political analyst to city council member and now city council president.

She didn't believe it, she couldn't possibly believe it. Her father didn't have financial problems. In fact, she knew for certain that he was solvent. It was she who reconciled his bank statements because Isaac Mixon didn't want to have anything to do with money. He was an ideas person, not a numbers guy. In fact, he was a political genius when it came to political campaign strategies.

"I don't believe you," she told the well-dressed man with a sallow pockmarked complexion. It was almost impossible to discern the color of his eyes behind a pair of thick lenses perched on a short nose that gave him a porcine appearance.

"Perhaps Councilman Cooper and I should leave you alone with your father for a few moments so he can bare his soul. Perhaps then you'll believe me."

Thomas nodded to Zabrina. "Mr. Davidson and I will be in your father's study. Please, don't get up. I know where it is."

Zabrina felt her throat closing as a wave of rage held her captive, not permitting her to draw a normal breath. It was the second time the arrogant politician had usurped her in her home. Once she'd reached sixteen she'd thought of the three-bedroom condo as *hers*. It was then that she'd assumed the responsibility of mistress of the house when standing in as hostess for Isaac Mixon's many political confabs and soirées.

She drew in a breath and closed her eyes. When she opened them and stared at her father he seemed to have aged within a matter of seconds. "What's going on, Daddy?"

Isaac Mixon knew whatever he'd been instructed to tell his daughter was going to destroy her. But either he had to lie or go to jail for a crime he did not commit. And disclosing what he knew meant his chances of survival were slim to none. Thomas Cooper had too many connections in *and* out of prison.

He walked across the living room and sank down on a love seat. "I'm sorry, baby girl, I—"

"You're sorry, Daddy!" Zabrina hadn't realized she was screaming, and at her father no less. "You're sorry for what?"

"I did divert some of Tom's campaign funds."

"Divert or steal, Daddy?"

Isaac saw fire in his daughter's eyes, the same fire that had burned so brightly in her mother's eyes before a debilitating disease had stolen her spirit and will to live. Zabrina had inherited Jacinta's palomino-gold coloring, inky-black hair and hazel eyes that always reminded him of semi-precious jewels. He hadn't celebrated his tenth wedding anniversary when he lost his wife, but fate hadn't taken everything from him because Jacinta lived on in the image of their daughter.

"I took the money," he lied smoothly.

"But why did you do it? You have money."

Isaac lowered his salt-and-pepper head, focusing his attention on the thick pile of the carpet under his feet. He knew if he met his daughter's eyes he wouldn't be able to continue to lie to her. "I...I've been gambling—"

"But you never gamble!"

"But I do now!" he spat out in a nasty tone. "I bet on everything: cards, ponies and even illegal numbers."

Zabrina's eyelids fluttered as she tried processing what her father was telling her. "Why didn't you use your own money?"

He glared at her. "I didn't want you to know about my nasty little addiction."

"How much did you take?"

"Eighty-three," Isaac admitted.

"Eighty-three...eighty-three hundred," Zabrina repeated over and over. "I have more than that in my savings account. I'll go to the bank tomorrow and get a bank check payable to Thomas Cooper—"

"Stop, Brina! It's not eighty-three hundred but eighty-three thousand—money Tom gave me to pay off loan sharks who'd threatened to kill me." Tears filled Isaac Mixon's eyes as his face crumpled like an accordion. "I took twenty thousand from the campaign fund and borrowed the rest from a loan shark. "Right now I owe Thomas Cooper more than one hundred thousand dollars."

"What about the money in your 401K?" she asked.

"I'll have to pay it back," Isaac said.

"How about selling the condo?"

Isaac shook his head. "That would take too long."

Zabrina's eyes narrowed. "How much time has Thomas given you to repay him without pressing charges?"

"He wants my answer now."

"Answer to what, Daddy?"

Isaac's head came up and he met his daughter's eyes for the first time, seeing pain and unshed tears. "Thomas has threatened to have me arrested unless I can get you to agree to…" His words trailed off.

Zabrina leaned forward. "Get me to do what?"

"He wants you to marry him."

Her father's words hit her like a punch to the face, and for a brief moment she believed he was joking, blurting out anything that came to mind to belie his fear. Her hands tightened on the arms of the chair.

"Thomas Cooper wants to marry me when he knows I'm going to marry another man in two weeks?" Isaac nodded. "I can't, Daddy!" She was screaming again.

Isaac pushed to his feet. The droop of his shoulders indicated defeat. His so-called protégé was blackmailing him because of what he'd witnessed when he'd walked into Thomas's private office: Councilman Cooper had accepted a cash payment from a local Philadelphia businessman whom law officials suspected had ties to organized crime.

It was a week later that a strange man was ushered into Isaac's office with a message from the businessman: *forget what you saw or your daughter will find herself placing flowers on her father's grave.*

Later that evening he'd met with Thomas who had made him an offer he couldn't refuse. The confirmed bachelor talked incessantly about enhancing his image before declaring his candidacy for the mayoralty race, and then had shocked Isaac when he told him that he wanted to marry his daughter. Nothing Isaac could say could dissuade Cooper even when he told Thomas that Zabrina was engaged to marry Myles Eaton. Thomas Cooper dismissed the pronouncement with a wave of his hand, claiming marrying Zabrina Mixon would serve as added insurance that her father would never turn on his son-in-law.

Zabrina didn't, couldn't move. "I don't believe this. This is the twenty-first century, yet you're offering me up as if I were chattel you'd put up in a card game. I could possibly consider marrying Thomas if I wasn't engaged or pregnant. But, I'm sorry, Daddy. I can't."

Isaac turned slowly and stared down at his daughter's bowed head. "You're what?"

Her head came up. "I just found out this morning that I'm pregnant with Myles Eaton's baby."

"Does he know?" Isaac's voice was barely a whisper.

"Not yet. I plan to tell him later tonight."

"But you won't tell him, Zabrina. The child will carry my name," said Thomas confidently.

Zabrina hadn't realized Thomas and the other man he'd called Davidson had reentered the living room. "Go to hell!"

The elected official's expression did not change. "Mr. Davidson, perhaps you can convince Miss Mixon of the seriousness of her father's dilemma."

The bespectacled man reached under his suit jacket, pulled out a small caliber handgun with a silencer, aiming it at Isaac's head. "You have exactly five seconds, Miss Mixon, to give Councilman Cooper an answer."

Zabrina's heart was beating so hard she was certain it could be seen through her blouse. "Okay!" she screamed. "Okay," she repeated, this time her acquiescence softer. There was no mistaking defeat in the single word.

Thomas smiled for the first time. "Not only are you beautiful, but you're very, very smart. We'll marry next week in a private ceremony. And, you don't have to worry about me exercising my conjugal rights. Our marriage will be in name only."

A rage she'd never known burned through Zabrina. "Does that leave me free to take a lover or lovers?"

The councilman's smile faded. "In two years you'll be the wife of Philadelphia's next mayor, so I doubt that with the responsibility of raising a child and taking care of your social obligations, you'll find time to open your legs to another man."

She felt the overwhelming sick feeling that came with defeat, but she wasn't going to let the blackmailing SOB know that. "One of these days I'm going to kill you."

A slight arch in his eyebrows was the only indication that Thomas had registered her threat. "Take a number, Miss Mixon." He motioned to his gofer to put the gun away. "I suggest you call your *fiancé* and tell him you found a better prospect."

The footsteps of the two men were muffled in the carpet

as they turned and walked to the door. The solid slam of the door shocked Zabrina into an awareness of just what had taken place within a matter of minutes. She'd agreed to marry a man she'd come to detest when the baby of another man she'd pledged to marry in two weeks was growing beneath her heart.

She registered another sound, and it took her several seconds to realize her father was crying. Even when they'd buried her mother she hadn't seen Isaac cry. She stood up and walked over to her father. Going to her knees, Zabrina pressed her face to his chest. It wasn't easy to comfort him when she was sobbing inconsolably.

It was later, much later when Zabrina retreated to her bedroom to call Myles Eaton to tell him that she couldn't marry him because she was in love with another man. There was only the sound of breathing coming through the earpiece until a distinctive click told her Myles had hung up.

She didn't cry only because she had no more tears. Her mind was a maelstrom of thoughts that ranged from premeditated murder to the need to survive to bring her unborn child to term. She may have lost Myles Eaton, but unknowingly he'd given her a precious gift—a gift she would love to her dying breath.

Chapter 3

Ten years later...

"I can't believe you're marrying your sister's brother-in-law."

"Believe it, because in another week I'll become Mrs. Griffin Rice."

A hint of a smile lifted the corners of Belinda Eaton's mouth as she stared at Zabrina Cooper. As she'd promised when she'd run into Zabrina at a fundraiser, she'd called to set up a dinner date with the woman who at one time had been engaged to her brother.

Her twin nieces, Layla and Sabrina, whom she and Griffin legally adopted after their parents died in a horrific head-on automobile accident, were spending the weekend with their paternal grandparents, giving Belinda the time she needed to meet with her childhood friend and finish packing her personal belongings before she moved into Griffin's house. They had gone from being godparents to parents, after Belinda's sister, who was married to Griffin's brother, died tragically in an auto accident, leaving the twins orphans.

The skin around Zabrina's large light brown eyes crinkled when she smiled, something she hadn't done often, or in a very long time. The only person who could get her to smile or laugh spontaneously was her son. Adam was not only the love of her life, he was her life. Her mother had died when she was young, and she'd buried her father four months before she'd become a widow. Aside from an aunt and a few distant cousins there was only Adam.

She sobered, staring at the woman who, if she'd married Myles Eaton, would have become her sister-in-law. To say the high-school history teacher was stunning was an understatement. The soft glow from the candle on the table flattered Belinda's flawless sable complexion. A little makeup accentuated the exotic slant of her dark eyes, high cheekbones, short straight nose and generously curved full mouth. A profusion of dark curly hair framed her attractive face.

Zabrina's gaze moved from Belinda's face to her hand, which flaunted a magnificent emerald-cut diamond ring surrounded with baguettes. She remembered the engagement ring Myles had slipped on her finger, a ring she had returned to him via a bonded messenger hours after she'd called him to let him know she couldn't marry him because she was in love with another man.

"I knew there was something going on between you and Griffin when you two were maid of honor and best man at

Donna and Grant's wedding." Belinda's older sister had married Griffin's older brother.

Belinda took a sip from her water goblet. "That's where you're wrong, Brina. Griffin and I barely tolerated each other. What I hadn't realized at the time was that I was in love with him. But instead of letting him know that, I acted like a junior-high schoolgirl who punches out the boy so everyone believes that she despises rather than likes him."

Zabrina stared at her bare hands resting on the table-cloth. "It was the same with me and Myles. He used to tease me mercilessly until I kissed him. I don't know who was more shocked—me or him."

"You kissed my brother first?"

Zabrina's face became flushed as she cast her eyes downward. "He was leaving for college, and I didn't want him to forget me."

"And apparently he didn't," Belinda said softly.

Zabrina looked up and her eyes met Belinda's. "I was thirteen when I kissed Myles for the first time, and I had to wait another five years before he kissed me back. Myles claimed he didn't want to take advantage of a minor, so he felt at eighteen I was old enough either to let him kiss me or punch his lights out." Her eyes brimmed with tears. "The happiest day in my life was when your brother asked me to marry him and one of the darkest was when I called to tell him I was in love with another man."

Reaching across the table, Belinda placed her hand over Zabrina's ice-cold fingers. "What happened, Brina? I know you loved my brother, so why did you lie to him?"

The seconds ticked off as the two women stared at each other. They'd met in the first grade and become fast friends.

Then tragedy had separated them for a year when Zabrina's mother was diagnosed with brain cancer.

Isaac Mixon moved his wife and daughter to Mexico for an experimental treatment not approved by oncologists in the United States. Zabrina had just celebrated her seventh birthday when Jacinta passed away. Her body was cremated and her ashes scattered in the ocean.

Zabrina returned to the States with her father, not to live in the stately white Colonial with black trim but in a three-bedroom condominium in an exclusive Philadelphia neighborhood. She and Belinda no longer attended the same school, yet they'd managed to get together every weekend. Belinda would either stay over at Zabrina's, or she would sleep over at Belinda's. Though Belinda had two other sisters, Zabrina Mixon had become her best friend *and* unofficial sister. But a lifetime of friendship had ended with a single telephone call to Myles Eaton.

Belinda stared at the beautiful woman with the gold-brown skin, gleaming black chin-length hair and brilliant hazel eyes. She remembered photographs of Jacinta Mixon, and Zabrina was her mother's twin.

"I had to, Belinda," Zabrina said in a soft voice. "I wasn't given a choice."

"Who didn't give you a choice, Brina?"

Zabrina averted her gaze, staring out the restaurant window at the patrons dining alfresco in the warm June temperatures. "It had to do with my father." Her gaze swung back to Belinda and she closed her eyes for several seconds. "I've already said too much."

"Are you saying you were forced to marry Thomas Cooper?"

"The only other thing I'm going to say is I didn't want

to marry Thomas. Please, Belinda, don't ask me any more questions, because I can't answer them."

She'd promised her father she would never tell anyone what he'd done although she was tempted to do just that after burying Isaac Mixon. However, she'd changed her mind when she thought of how it would've affected Adam. Her son idolized his grandfather.

"You can't or you won't?"

"I can't."

Their waiter approached the table, bringing the difficult conversation to an end. The two women ordered, then settled back to discuss Belinda's upcoming wedding.

Belinda touched a napkin to the corners of her mouth. "I know you sent back your response card saying you're coming, but I want to warn you that Myles will also be there. He came in from Pittsburgh last night and plans to spend the summer here in Philly."

Zabrina nodded. She'd had more than ten years to prepare to meet Myles Eaton again. Marrying Thomas Cooper would've been akin to a death sentence if not for her son. Raising Adam had kept her sane, rational and out of prison.

"It's been a long time, but I've known eventually we would have to come face-to-face with each other one of these days." She couldn't predict what Myles's reaction would be to seeing her again, but she was certain he would find her a very different woman from the one who'd pledged to love him forever.

The two women talked about old friends, jokes they'd played on former classmates and the boys they'd had crushes on but who hadn't given them a single glance. They talked about everything except the loss of their loved ones—Belinda's sister and brother-in-law and Zabrina's parents.

Both declined dessert and coffee. "Who's your maid of honor?" Zabrina asked.

Belinda wanted to tell Zabrina *she* would've been her matron of honor if she had married Myles. "Chandra. She's scheduled to fly in Monday, because she has to be fitted for her dress." Belinda's sister had joined the Peace Corps and was currently teaching in Belize. "My cousin Denise will be my other attendant. Myles will stand in as Griffin's best man and Keith Ennis will be a groomsman."

With wide eyes, Zabrina whispered, "Baseball player Keith Ennis?"

Belinda smiled. "Yes. He's one of Griffin's clients." Her fiancé was the lawyer for half a dozen superstar athletes.

"It looks as if you're going to have quite the celebrity wedding."

"All I want is for it to be over, so that my life can return to normal."

"Are you going on a honeymoon?" Zabrina asked.

"Yes. We're going to spend two weeks at a private villa on St. Kitts. I plan to sleep late, take in the sun and eat and drink until I can't move."

Zabrina smiled again, then her smile vanished when she spied the man she hadn't expected to see until Belinda's wedding. Myles Adam Eaton had walked into the restaurant with a beautiful, petite dark-skinned woman with her hand draped possessively over the sleeve of his suit jacket. Myles immediately glanced in her direction. Their eyes met, recognition dawned and then the moment passed when he dipped his head to listen to something the woman was saying. To say time had been kind to Myles was an understatement. Quickly averting her gaze so Belinda wouldn't see what had gotten her attention, she signaled for the waiter.

"I'll take the check please."

Zabrina silently applauded herself for becoming quite
the accomplished actress. It'd taken a decade of smiling
when she hadn't wanted to smile, uttering the appropriate
phrases and responses when attending political events,
even though she'd wanted to spew expletives. She didn't
know if the woman on Myles's arm was his wife, fiancée
or date for the evening, but it didn't matter. Zabrina didn't
ever expect to become Mrs. Myles Eaton. Having his son
was her consolation for having to give him up.

"I told you I was treating tonight," Belinda said between
clenched teeth.

Zabrina took the leather binder from the waiter. "You
can treat the next time."

She didn't tell Belinda that with all of Thomas Cooper's
so-called political and legal savvy he'd neglected to draw
up a will, and she'd inherited a multimillion-dollar home,
which she'd promptly sold, and investments of which
she'd had no previous knowledge. She'd sold the shares
before Wall Street bottomed out and deposited the proceeds into an account for her son's education. Becoming
a wealthy woman was a huge price to pay for having to
give up the man she loved while denying her son his birthright.

Zabrina settled the bill, pushed back her chair and
walked out of the restaurant, Belinda following, without
glancing over to where Myles sat with his dinner date. She
waited with Belinda for the parking attendants to retrieve
their cars from valet parking. Her car arrived first.

She hugged her childhood friend. "I'll see you next week."

"Next week," Belinda repeated.

Zabrina got into her late-model Lincoln sedan and maneuvered out of the restaurant parking lot. She hadn't realized her hands were shaking until she stopped for a red light. She closed her eyes, inhaling a lungful of cool air flowing from the automobile's air conditioner. When she opened her eyes the light had changed and she was back in control.

Myles Eaton pretended to be interested in the menu on the table in front of him to avoid staring at the table where Zabrina Mixon and his sister had been. A wry smile touched his mouth. He'd forgotten. She was no longer a Mixon. She was now Zabrina Cooper.

As an attorney and professor of constitutional law, he'd memorized countless Supreme Court decisions, yet he had not, could not, did not want to remember the dozen words that had turned his world upside down.

His fiancée, the woman to whom he'd pledged his life and his future had waited until two weeks before they were to be married to call and tell him she couldn't marry him because she was in love with another man. And when he'd discovered the "other man" was none other than Thomas Cooper, his rage had escalated until he realized he had to leave Philadelphia or spend the rest of his life obsessing about the woman who'd broken his heart.

Thomas Cooper used every opportunity to parade and flaunt his much younger wife. Myles could still recall the photographs of a very pregnant Zabrina with the councilman's hand splayed over her swollen belly at a fundraiser. Then there was the official family photograph with the haunted look in Zabrina's eyes when she'd stared directly into the camera lens. There were rumors that she'd been afflicted with chronic postpartum depression, while others hinted that marital problems had beset the Coopers and they were seeing a marriage counselor.

All of the rumors ended for Myles when he requested and was granted a transfer to work out of the law firm's New York office. Adjusting to the faster pace of New York had been the balm he needed to start over. The cramped studio apartment was a far cry from his spacious condo. But that hadn't been important, because most nights when he came home after putting in a fourteen-hour day he'd shower and fall into bed, then get up and do it all over again.

He'd given New York City eight years of his life before he decided he didn't want to practice law, but teach it. He contacted a former professor who told him of an opening at his law-school alma mater. He applied for the position, went through the interview process and when he received the letter of appointment to teach constitutional law at Duquesne's law school in Pittsburgh, he finally found peace.

"What are you having, Myles?"

His head jerked up and he smiled at the woman who'd become his law-school mentor. Judge Stacey Greer-Monroe had graduated from high school at fifteen, college at eighteen and law school two months after her twenty-first birthday. Myles thought Stacey was one of the most brilliant legal minds he'd ever encountered, including his professors.

"I think I'm going to order the crab cakes."

"What's the matter, Professor Eaton? You can't get good crab cakes in Steel City?" Stacey joked.

His smile grew wider. "I get the best Maryland-style crab cakes west of the Alleghenies at a little restaurant owned by a woman who moved from Baltimore. Sadie G's has become my favorite eating place."

Stacey lowered her gaze rather than stare openly at the

man she'd tried unsuccessfully to get to think of her as
more than a friend. But their every encounter ended with
a hug and a kiss on the cheek. After he was jilted by his
fiancée Myles continued to regard Stacey as friend and
peer. Their relationship remained the same after he'd
moved to New York and then Pittsburgh when they communicated with each other online.

Stacey's hopes of becoming Mrs. Myles Eaton ended
when her biological clock began winding down and she
married a neurosurgeon she'd dated off and on for years.
She was now the mother of a two-year-old daughter.

"So, you're really serious about putting down roots in
Pittsburgh?"

Myles's dark eyebrows framed his eyes in a lean
mahogany-brown angular face that once seen wasn't easily
forgotten. "I've been house-hunting," he admitted. The
one-year lease on his rental would expire at the end of
August. "And I've seen a few places I happen to like."

Stacey angled her head. "I thought you'd prefer a
condo or co-op."

"I'd thought so, too. But after living in apartments the
past nine years I'm looking to spread out. I don't like en-
tertaining only a few feet from where I have to sleep."

"You could buy a duplex."

Myles studied Stacey's face, one of the youngest jurists
elected to Philadelphia's Supreme Court. Stacey Greer-
Monroe had always reminded him of a fragile doll. But under
the soft, delicate exterior was a tough but fair judge. Her
grandfather was a judge, as was her father. And Stacey had
continued the tradition when she was elected to the bench.

"I miss waking up to the smell of freshly cut grass and
firing up the grill during the warm weather."

Stacey smiled. "It sounds as if you're ready to settle down and become a family man."

Myles wanted to tell her he'd been ready to settle down ten years before. Then he'd looked forward to marrying Zabrina and raising a family, but that changed when she'd married Thomas Cooper and gave him the son that should've been theirs.

"Excuse me, Judge Monroe, but are you ready to order a cocktail?"

Frowning slightly, Stacey shifted her attention from Myles to their waiter. Talk about bad timing. She was just about to ask him whether he was seeing a woman, and, if he was, was it serious? "Yes." She smiled at Myles. "Do you mind if I order a bottle of champagne to celebrate your return to Philly?"

"Not at all, Judge."

He'd come back to Philadelphia to spend the summer and reconnect with his family. He'd checked into a hotel downtown for the week. After the wedding he would move into Belinda's house for the summer. His sister hadn't decided whether she wanted to sell or rent her house. It was to be the first time in a decade that he'd spend more than a few days with his parents, siblings and nieces.

Waiting until the man walked away, Stacey said to Myles, "I told you never to call me that!"

"Aren't you a judge, Stacey?"

"Yes, but only in the courtroom."

"I've never known you to be self-deprecating. When we met for the first time all you talked about was becoming a judge."

"I was all of twenty-six and I wanted to impress my very bright protégé. You had to know that I liked you."

"And I told you I was in love with someone else," Myles countered.

A beat passed. "Are you still in love with her, Myles?"

His eyebrows flickered before settling back into place. "Yes," he admitted truthfully. "A part of me will always love her."

Stacey curbed the urge to reach across the table to grasp Myles's hand. "I'm glad I married when I did, because I'd still be waiting for you to notice me."

He angled his head and stared directly at his dining partner. "I noticed you, Stacey, only because you were trying too hard. The flirtatious looks, the indiscriminate touching and the occasional kiss on the lips instead of the cheek were obvious."

Stacey's lashes fluttered as she tried to bring her emotions under control. She'd always thought she'd been subtle in her attempts to seduce Myles Eaton, but evidently she had been anything but. "You knew?"

He nodded. "I knew, and I promise I won't tell your husband."

"You must have thought me a real idiot."

Reaching across the table, Myles covered her hand with his. "No, Stacey. We weren't that different. We both wanted someone we couldn't have."

He'd wanted Zabrina at eighteen, and at thirty-eight he still wanted her.

Chapter 4

It was a picture-perfect day in late June when two ushers opened the French doors and Dr. Dwight Eaton escorted his daughter over a pink runner monogrammed in green with the couple's initials. Light and dark pink rose petals littering the runner had been placed there by the bride's nieces wearing pink-and-green dresses and headbands with green button mums and pink nerines, the colors representing Belinda's sorority, Alpha Kappa Alpha.

The one hundred and twenty guests, welcomed with champagne and caviar into a Bucks County château built on a rise that overlooked the Delaware River, stood as the intro to the *Wedding March* filled the room where the ceremony was to take place. The restored castle and all of the estate's thirty-two rooms were filled with out-of-town guests and those who didn't want to make the hour-long drive back to Philadelphia after a night of frivolity.

Zabrina felt her heart lurch when she saw Belinda. Her childhood friend and sorority sister was ravishing in an ivory Chantilly lace empire gown with a floral appliqué-and-satin bodice. Embroidered petals flowed around the sweeping hem and train of the ethereal garment. She'd forgone a veil in lieu of tiny white rosebuds pinned into the elegant chignon on the nape of her long, graceful neck.

At that moment Zabrina was reliving her past—she should have walked down the aisle on her father's arm as Myles waited to make her his wife. Blinking back tears, she stared at his distinctive profile as he stood on Griffin Rice's right.

She noticed changes she hadn't been able to discern the week before. His face was thinner, there were flecks of gray in his close-cropped hair and there was a stubborn set to his lean jaw that made him appear as if he'd been carved from a piece of smooth, dark mahogany. Her gaze dropped to his left hand. She smiled. He wasn't wearing a ring.

Zabrina had searched her memory for days until she matched the face of the woman clinging to Myles's arm with a name. The woman was Judge Stacey Greer-Monroe.

She smiled when the rich, deep voice of the black-robed judge punctuated the silence. Griffin Rice, devastatingly handsome in formal attire, stared directly into the eyes of his bride as he repeated his vows. There was a twitter of laughter when the judge pronounced them husband and wife and Griffin pumped his fist in the air. It was over. Belinda was now Mrs. Belinda Rice.

The wedding party proceeded along the carpet to the reception. Zabrina didn't notice Belinda, Griffin, Keith Ennis, Chandra or Denise Eaton. Her gaze was fixed on Myles as he came closer and closer, and then their eyes met and fused. His eyes grew wider as a wry smile parted his firm lips.

The smile, Myles and his powerful presence were there. Then they vanished as he moved past her. Emerging from her trance, she followed the crowd as the hotel staff ushered everyone down a wide tunnel that led outside where an enormous tent had been erected. Belinda and Griffin stood in a receiving line, greeting family members and friends who'd come to witness and celebrate their special day.

Belinda's eyebrows shot up when she saw her friend. Zabrina had cut her hair in a style that drew one's attention to her luminous eyes. Raven-black waves were brushed off her face. The style would've been too severe for some with less delicate features. She was stunning in a silk chiffon off-the-shoulder black dress that hugged her upper body, nipping her slender waist with a wide silk sash before flaring around her knees. Stilettos added several inches to her impressive five-foot-seven-inch height.

"You look incredible," Belinda gushed.

"Thank you. And you're an amazing bride, Lindy."

Zabrina stole a glance at Griffin Rice as he leaned down to whisper something in the ear of an elderly woman who giggled like a teenage girl. She'd thought him breathtakingly handsome when she was a teenager, and her opinion hadn't changed. His deep-set dark eyes and cleft chin had most women lusting after him. But Griffin had always seemed totally oblivious to their attention. It was apparent he'd been waiting for his brother's sister-in-law.

Griffin turned his attention to Zabrina. She looked nothing like the young woman he remembered. "Thank you for coming." Leaning forward, he pressed a light kiss to her cheek.

"Thank you for inviting me." Zabrina knew she couldn't hold up the receiving line. "I'll be in touch with you guys after you come back from your honeymoon." When she'd married Thomas Cooper he'd made certain to isolate her from everyone in her past.

"Your name, miss?" asked a hotel staffer as she stood in front of a table stacked with butler boxes.

"Zabrina Cooper."

He handed her a box. "Your table number and menu are in the box, Ms. Cooper."

In lieu of a guest card, each guest was given a personalized butler box with a leaf-colored letterpressed menu and table number. The pink-and-green color scheme was repeated in the pastel-toned chiffon on the ceiling of the tent, table linens and carpet. The lights from strategically placed chandeliers provided a soft glow as the afternoon sun cast shadows over the elegantly dressed guests as they found their way to their respective tables.

Waiters were positioned at each table to pull out chairs and assist everyone as they sat on pink-cushioned bamboo-gilded chairs. And because Zabrina had returned her response card for one, she was seated at a table with other single guests. She offered a smile to the two men flanking her. The one on her right extended his hand.

"Bailey Mercer."

She stared at the young man with flaming red hair and blue-green eyes, then took his hand. It was soft and moist. As discreetly as she could without offending him, she withdrew her hand. "It's nice meeting you, Bailey. I'm Zabrina."

He draped an arm over the back of her chair. "Are you a guest of the bride or the groom?"

"The bride," she said.

"Are you a teacher?"

"No. I'm a nurse." Zabrina realized he just wanted to

make polite conversation. "Are you a guest of the bride or groom?" she asked.

"Griffin and I were college roommates."

"Are you also an attorney?"

Bailey leaned closer. "I'm a forensic criminologist."

Suddenly her curiosity was piqued. "Who do you work for?"

"I'm stationed in Quantico."

"You work for the Bureau?" she asked. The FBI was the only law-enforcement agency that she knew of in Quantico, Virginia.

Bailey nodded. "I'm going to the bar to get something to drink. Would you like me to bring you something?"

Zabrina smiled. He'd segued from one topic to another without pausing to take a breath. "Yes, please."

"What would you like?"

"I'll have a cosmopolitan."

Music from speakers mounted overhead filled the tent as guests filed in and sat at their assigned tables. Bailey returned with Zabrina's cocktail and a glass filled with an amber liquid. Smiling, they touched glasses.

Myles returned from posing for photographs with the wedding party to find Zabrina smiling and talking to a man with strawberry-blond hair. Sitting at the bridal table afforded him an unobscured view of everything and everyone in the large tent.

There was something in the way she angled her head while staring up at the man through her lashes that reminded him of how she'd look at him just before he'd make love to her. It was a come-hither look that he hadn't been able to resist.

What Myles hadn't been able to understand was how he and Zabrina were able to communicate without words. It could be a single glance, a slight lifting of an eyebrow, a shrug of a shoulder or a smile. It was as if they were able to communicate telepathically, reading each other's thoughts. Right now he knew she would be shocked if she saw the lust in his eyes. The spell was broken when a waiter took his dinner and beverage request.

"I almost didn't recognize Zabrina," said Griffin Rice.

Myles gave his brother-in-law a sidelong glance. "She *has* changed." And he wanted to tell Griffin the change was for the better. When he'd caught a glimpse of Zabrina the week before he'd thought her lovely, but tonight she was breathtakingly stunning.

Griffin's gaze met and fused with Myles's. "She'd dropped out of sight for years. Rumors were circulating that she and Cooper had divorced. But when reporters asked him about his wife he claimed she preferred keeping a low profile."

Myles's eyes narrowed slightly. "Who's the guy with her?"

"Bailey Mercer. We were college roomies."

The smile that softened Myles's mouth crept up to his eyes. It was apparent Zabrina had come to the wedding unescorted. He'd planned to ask her to dance with him and nothing more, since he hadn't wanted to act inappropriately *if* she had come with a date. Now that he knew she was alone things had changed. Myles had waited ten years for an explanation for Zabrina's deception *and* he intended to get an answer before the night ended.

The waiter brought drinks for those at the bridal party table, followed by other waitstaff carrying trays laden with platters of curried scallop canapés, walnut and endive salad and mushroom rolls. Dozens of lighted votives in green glasses flickered like stars when the chandeliers were dimmed, creating a soft, soothingly romantic atmosphere.

Myles ate without actually tasting the food on his plate. He was too engrossed in the woman sitting close enough for him to see her expressions, but not close enough to hear her smoky voice. He wondered if Griffin's former college roommate was as enthralled with her as he'd been. What he did do was drink more than he normally would at a social function. It didn't matter, because he wasn't driving back to Philadelphia. He'd reserved a suite at the hotel.

And, he refused to fantasize that his sister's wedding was his and Zabrina's. He and Zabrina had planned their wedding, honeymoon and life together, but all the plans had come to naught two weeks before the ceremony when his fiancée called to tell him she was in love with another man and she couldn't marry him.

Myles still remembered her passion whenever they shared a bed, and wondered whether she'd screamed Thomas Cooper's name in the throes of passion. Zabrina had always had an intense distaste for politicians. Yet she'd married one. And what about her claim that she'd wanted to wait two years before starting a family? She'd wasted no time in giving Cooper a child.

The music playing throughout the dinner ended when a live band took over, playing softly as toasts to the bride and groom were made.

Dwight Eaton wiped away tears as he smiled at his daughter. There was no doubt he was thinking of his eldest daughter whom he'd buried eight months earlier. Myles toasted the newlyweds, providing a lighter moment when he reminded everyone that Griffin Rice was so intent on joining the family that he'd become his brother-in-law for the second time.

A hush descended over the assembly as they watched Griffin ease Belinda to her feet, escort her to the dance floor and dance with her to the Berlin classic "Take My Breath Away." It was their first dance as husband and wife.

Myles finally got to twirl his sister around the dance floor after she'd shared a dance with their father. "Does Griffin know he is a lucky man?" he asked, executing a fancy dance step.

Belinda lifted the skirt of her gown to avoid stepping on the hem. She gave Myles a demure smile. "I'd like to believe that I'm lucky that Griffin didn't marry some other woman, leaving me pining for him for the rest of my life."

Myles recalled the conversation he'd had with Stacey. She'd waited for him to come around and think of her as more than a friend, and when it hadn't happened she'd opted to marry someone else. He was certain his sister would've done the same.

"You're too much of a realist to spend your life dreaming of the impossible."

Belinda smiled at Myles. "What about you and Brina?"

A slight frown furrowed his forehead. "What about us?"

"You still have feelings for her, don't you?"

"Of course I have feelings for her, Lindy. After all, I did promise to marry the woman."

"What about now, Myles?"

"What about it?" he said, answering her question with one of his own.

Belinda gasped softly when Myles swung her around and around. Her brother had always been a very good dancer, and it appeared that he hadn't lost his skill. She wasn't certain whether his dancing prowess came from years of martial arts training or from a natural grace and style that turned heads whenever he entered a room. Although he'd earned a black belt in tae kwon do, he intensely disliked competition.

Belinda leaned closer, pressing her mouth to his ear. "You haven't taken your eyes off her all night."

Myles's expression did not change. "Is that why you invited her, Lindy? Did you decide to become a matchmaker after I'd agreed to be Griffin's best man? Don't you think she hurt our family enough when she waited until two weeks before we were to be married to tell me that she was in love with someone else? Then, a week later she marries Thomas Cooper."

"I didn't invite her to spite you, Myles. It was only a couple of months ago that I ran into Brina for the first time in almost ten years. When she confessed that she hated Thomas Cooper as much as she loved you, I knew something wasn't quite right."

A sardonic smile spread across his face. "So, she lied twice. Once when she told me that she was in love with another man, and again when she tells you that she hated her husband."

Belinda shook her head. "It's all too confusing. When I asked her why she'd married Thomas, she said she couldn't tell me. She mentioned something about swearing that she'd never tell anyone."

"Swore to whom?"

"That I don't know, Myles."

The song ended and Myles led Belinda back to her seat beside her husband. He'd heard enough. He needed answers. He wanted answers and he intended to get them.

His gaze searched the crowded dance floor for Zabrina, but she was nowhere in sight. She was missing and so was Griffin's college roommate. There was no doubt they were together. Wending his way across the tent, Myles stepped out into the warm night air.

Chairs and love seats were set up on the verdant lawn for those wishing to get away from the frivolity to sit, talk quietly and/or relax. Dozens of lanterns were suspended from stanchions surrounding the magnificent estate. He saw Zabrina with her red-haired dining partner sitting together on a love seat. She'd rested her head on his shoulder while he massaged her back.

Taking long strides, Myles approached the couple. "Is she all right?"

Bailey Mercer glanced up to find the groom's best man looming over him like an avenging angel. "Zabrina said she needed some air."

Myles hunkered down and placed the back of his hand against her moist cheek. "Brina, darling, are you all right?" The endearment had slipped out as if ten years had morphed into a nanosecond.

Zabrina heard the familiar voice from her past, and she tried smiling but the pounding in her temples intensified. "I don't know."

"What did she eat or drink?" Myles asked Bailey.

"She didn't eat much, but she did have three cocktails."

Effortlessly, Myles lifted Zabrina off the love seat, while coming to a standing position. "She can't drink."

Bailey stood up. "What the hell are you talking about?"

"She usually can't have more than one drink or she'll wind up with a headache."

"I'll take care of her," Bailey offered.

Myles glared at the man. "Walk away."

A flush suffused Bailey's face, the color increasing to match his hairline. He moved closer. "I said I'll take care of her."

Myles angled his head. "Don't get in my face," he warned through clenched teeth. "Look, man," he said, his tone softer, calmer. "Just walk away while you can." That said, he turned on his heels and carried Zabrina past the tent and into the hotel. He slipped in through a side entrance and took a staircase to the third floor. When he set Zabrina on her feet to search for his room's cardkey, she dropped her evening purse, spilling its contents.

"Muh—my things," Zabrina slurred.

"Don't worry about them, Brina. I'll pick them up after I get you inside."

Zabrina swallowed back a rush of bile. She felt sick, sicker than she had in a very long time. Her first experience with drinking alcohol had become a lasting one. But it was apparent she'd forgotten. She hadn't known what possessed her to have a third cosmopolitan. What she should've done was stop after the first one. But she'd wanted to forget that the past ten years hadn't existed. She wanted to blot them out by drinking until she passed out. She hadn't passed out, but she did have an excruciating headache.

Myles had always teased her, calling her a very cheap date. Her colleagues couldn't understand why she opted to drink club soda with a twist during their employee gatherings. Some had asked whether she was a recovering alcoholic, but she reassured them that she did drink, just always sparingly.

She closed her eyes as her dulled senses took over. Being cradled against Myles's broad chest brought back a rush of memories that made Zabrina want to weep. He'd always been there for her, had promised to love, protect and take care of her. He no longer loved her, yet he was still looking after her.

Myles walked through the entry, the living/dining area and into the bedroom. He placed Zabrina on the king-size bed, removed her shoes and covered her with a lightweight blanket. "I'll be right back."

He returned to the hall to gather up the jeweled compact, the tube of lipstick and a set of car keys that had fallen out of her bag. He pocketed the keys. Zabrina was in no shape to get behind the wheel of a car, even if just to drive it out of the parking lot. A cold chill swept over him when he thought of her trying to drive back to Philly under the circumstances. Either she would kill herself or someone else.

Closing the door, he slipped the security lock into place and returned to the bedroom. Zabrina hadn't moved. She lay on her back, eyes closed and her chest rising and falling in a slow, even rhythm. He smiled. She'd fallen asleep.

Myles reached up and undid his silk tie. Undressing, he placed his clothes on the padded bench at the foot of the bed. Clad in only a pair of boxer briefs, he retreated to the bathroom to shower and brush his teeth.

Zabrina was still asleep when Myles reentered the bedroom. She lay on her right side, her head resting on her hands and her legs pulled up into a fetal position. A smile tilted the corners of his mouth when he stared down at her. She was so incredibly beautiful and so very cunning. When he'd asked Zabrina to marry him he never would've thought she would deceive him, especially not with another man.

Reaching over, he turned off the bedside lamp. The light from the sconce outside the bathroom provided enough illumination to make out the slight figure on the bed. Sitting on the mattress, Myles studied the woman whom he'd never forgotten. He'd once admitted to Belinda that he had two passions—Zabrina Mixon and the law. Despite her deception, his feelings hadn't changed. Nothing had changed. Zabrina was still his passion.

Slowly, methodically, he undressed her. She stirred briefly before settling back to sleep. Waiting for her breathing to resume a measured cadence, he anchored a hand under her hips, easing her dress down her bare legs. Myles didn't know why, but he felt like a voyeur when he stared at Zabrina's half-naked body. She hadn't worn a bra under the dress. He recalled her preference for sleeping nude, but decided not to remove her bikini panties.

She moaned softly when he eased her between the sheets. He waited a full minute, then shrugged off his robe and slipped into bed beside her. It was as if nothing had changed. Pressing his chest to her back, he rested an arm over her waist, pulling her closer. The angry words Myles had rehearsed so many times he could recite them backward he'd erased from memory. He buried his face in her hair and inhaled the lingering floral fragrance of her shampoo.

"Myles?"

He froze when Zabrina whispered his name. "Yes, baby?"

"I…I…I'm sorry," she slurred.

There came a beat. "So am I," Myles whispered. "So am I, Brina," he repeated.

Myles wasn't certain what she was apologizing for, but he knew why he was sorry. He was sorry they hadn't gone through with their plan to marry, sorry that her son wasn't his and sorry it had taken almost a decade for him to get the opportunity to confront her about her deception.

Chapter 5

Zabrina knew something was different when she opened her eyes. She wasn't in her bed, *and* she wasn't alone. She sat up quickly, chiding herself for the sudden action. Her head felt as if it was in a vise, and her mouth was dry as sandpaper. She closed her eyes and sank back to the pillow.

"Are you all right?" asked a deep voice in the dimly lit space.

She didn't know if she was dreaming or hallucinating, because she couldn't believe she was in bed with Myles Eaton. "Is that you, Myles?"

The seconds ticked. "Yes, it is. Who were you expecting? Bailey Mercer?"

Turning over and pressing her face to the pillow, Zabrina muffled a moan. "That's not funny."

"What's not funny, Brina, is you drinking until you nearly passed out."

"I didn't pass out."

"No, but you were asleep before I got you into bed. You're lucky it was me and not your redheaded admirer. There was the possibility that he could've taken advantage of you."

Zabrina ignored the reference to the man who'd become her dinner partner. She sat up again, pulling the sheet up to her chin. "Where am I?"

"You're in my hotel room." Rolling over, Myles turned on the lamp on his side of the bed. The glowing numbers on the clock-radio read 1:22 a.m. "What time do you have to pick up your son?"

"Adam's in Virginia with my aunt's grandchildren."

Myles froze for a beat. He glanced over his shoulder to see the haunted golden eyes staring back at him. "You named Cooper's son Adam?"

A pregnant silence filled the space as Zabrina tried to form her thoughts. If she hadn't been under the influence she would've been able to spar verbally with Myles, but not now. She knew how persuasive he could be once he set his mind to something. That was what had made him an incredible trial attorney. He'd ask the same question ten different ways in an attempt to agitate and confuse a witness, and if she wasn't careful he would trip her up and uncover the truth about her son's paternity.

What frightened her most was Myles finding out that she'd had his child and passed it off as Thomas Cooper's. Although Adam's birth certificate listed Thomas Cooper as his father, Myles still had the law on his side if or when he decided to sue her for custody.

"I named *my* son Adam."

Myles ran a hand over his face. Zabrina had admitted to him that Adam was her favorite boy's name even before he'd told her it was his middle name. "Wasn't he also Cooper's son?"

"He was never Thomas's son. He was always too busy pressing the flesh and seeing to the needs of his constituents to play daddy even though Adam practically worshipped the ground Thomas walked on." She emitted a soft sigh. "I suppose not every man who's a father is father material."

"What about you, Brina?"

"What about me?"

"How are you coping with the loss of your husband?"

Zabrina's fingers tightened on the sheet clutched to her chest at the same time she affected a wry smile. "You see how I'm coping, Myles. I've become the merry widow. I know I can't handle more than one drink, but that didn't stop me from having three. That's how I'm coping," she spat out.

"Do you drink in front of your son?"

"You think I've become an alcoholic, don't you?"

Myles shook his head. "I didn't say that, Zabrina."

"But isn't that what you're implying, Myles?"

"No, it's not." Gathering the sheet, Zabrina tried getting out of bed, but Myles thwarted her attempt to escape him when his hand went around her upper arm. "Where do you think you're going?"

"I'm going home!"

One second she was sitting half on and half off the bed and within the next she found herself sprawled on her back, Myles straddling her. "I don't think so. Your son just lost his father. Do you want him to lose his mother, too?" He'd bared his teeth like a snarling canine. "If you try to walk out of here in the condition that you're in, then I'll call the police and have you locked up."

He hadn't wanted to remind Zabrina that less than a year

ago the Eatons and Rices had buried their daughter and son after they'd died in a head-on collision with a drunk driver. The loss of his sister and brother-in-law was devastating to both families. Whenever he returned to Philadelphia, Myles always expected to see Donna's inviting smile and infectious laughter.

Zabrina's eyes filled with tears and overflowed, tears she hadn't been able to shed after the police had arrived at her home to tell her that her husband had drowned in a boating accident off the Chesapeake. The media was respectful of her grief when told by the Coopers' housekeeper that the reclusive widow of Pennsylvania's junior senator was too distraught to conduct an interview. She'd gone into hiding again, resurfacing six months later at a fundraising event for mayoral candidate Patrick Garson.

She'd given Thomas Cooper nearly ten years of her life and six months was long enough for her to pretend to be the grieving widow. She didn't cry for Thomas because she didn't want to be a hypocrite. She hadn't lied to Belinda at the fundraiser when she'd told her that she hated Thomas as much as she loved her brother.

Cradling her face between his palms, Myles lowered his head and brushed his mouth over Zabrina's in an attempt to comfort her. "It's okay, baby. Let it out."

Zabrina had lost her father and husband, her son had lost his father and he knew her drinking too much was a feeble attempt to mask the pain. She wasn't weeping, but sobbing. Deep, gut-wrenching sobs that knifed through Myles like a rapier. Gathering her closer, he held her until the sobs faded into a soft hiccupping. He counted off the minutes until he heard the soft snores. Zabrina had fallen asleep.

As much as he loathed releasing her, Myles knew he couldn't spend the night straddling her body. Reluctantly, he lay beside Zabrina, holding her protectively as he joined her in sleep.

When Zabrina woke again she found herself in bed alone. The scent from Myles's cologne lingered but the heat from his body was missing. Sitting up and pulling the sheet to her breasts, she glanced around the room. Sunlight came through the lacy panels at a trio of tall windows.

The suite in the restored château hotel preserved a sense of family and intimacy. Furnished in French country decor with a four-poster bed, massive ornate armoire, triple dresser and mirror, and chairs with carved arms and petit-point cushions, it was a scene from *Dangerous Liaisons*.

Reaching for the black silk robe at the foot of the bed, she slipped into it and moved off the bed. Zabrina still didn't want to believe that she'd shared a bed with Myles Eaton. What she found laughable was that he was the only man she'd ever slept with. As promised, her marriage to Thomas had been in name only. They'd had adjoining bedroom suites, but Thomas had never exercised his conjugal rights, and that had become the best feature of their peculiar marriage.

At first she'd believed Thomas hadn't wanted to touch her because she was carrying another man's baby, but even after she'd given birth to her son, Thomas hadn't approached her. Zabrina didn't know what to make of her husband's sexual proclivity. She'd thought he preferred same-sex liaisons until she inadvertently discovered he'd been sleeping with his cousin's wife, and that her two sons weren't her husband's, but Thomas's. Zabrina didn't care who he slept with as long as he didn't try to consummate their sham of a marriage.

She walked into the bathroom, closing the door behind her. A low table held a supply of feminine grooming products along with a comb, toothbrush, toothpaste and mouthwash. She brushed her teeth and then stepped into the shower. Standing under the spray of a hot shower Zabrina swore never to overindulge again.

The smell of coffee met her when she emerged from the bathroom, her hair covered with a towel and her body swathed in black silk. She'd turned back the cuffs on the robe and looped the belt twice around her waist. However, there was little she could do with the lapels that kept slipping to reveal the tops of her breasts.

Myles walked into the bedroom at the same time she reached for her dress. "Breakfast is here. Come and eat."

Zabrina felt her pulse kick into a higher gear when she stared at the man who she couldn't remember ever *not* loving. Instead of the tuxedo from the night before, he wore a pair of faded jeans, running shoes, and a golf shirt that revealed solid pectorals and biceps.

"I'd like to put on some clothes."

Myles extended his hand. "You have clothes on, Brina. Come and eat before the food gets cold."

It was apparent he wasn't giving her much of a choice. And it wasn't that she *wasn't* hungry. The night before she'd elected to drink rather than eat, and Zabrina was certain that the lack of food had contributed to her feeling hungover. She approached Myles, placing her hand on his outstretched palm. He'd showered, but hadn't shaved and the stubble on his dark face enhanced his blatant masculinity.

Cradling the small hand in the crook of his elbow, Myles felt the fragility of the slender fingers. Although she'd had a child, her body was much slimmer than he'd remembered.

He pulled out her chair at the table in the dining area and then sat beside her. "How do you feel this morning?"

Zabrina gave him a sidelong glance. "A lot better than I did last night."

Myles gave her a warm smile. "Good." He gestured to her covered plate. "Eat, Brina."

She removed the cover and was tempted to salute him for telling her to eat. Myles had ordered a spinach omelet, bacon and a slice of buttered wheat toast for her. "You remembered my favorites." Her voice was barely a whisper.

Myles filled a glass with orange juice from a carafe, placing it in front of her plate. "I took a chance when I ordered it. People's tastes sometimes change."

Zabrina wanted to tell him she hadn't changed that much. Aside from having his son, her feelings for him hadn't changed. "Have you changed, Myles?"

Myles poured orange juice for himself. "Yes, I have. What has changed most are my priorities. Remember when all I talked about was making partner?"

She smiled. "Yes."

"After five years of working in New York, I finally made partner. After the announcement was made everyone at the firm got together at a restaurant to celebrate. But then when I woke up the next morning it was if nothing had changed. My name was added to the firm's plaque and letterhead and I moved into a large corner office. But I realized all of it was nothing more than vanity."

"That's the same with titles and awards," Zabrina said in a quiet voice as she speared a small portion of omelet.

"When all is said and done it's only vanity. It won't make you healthy, keep you out of jail or avoid death."

"My, my, my," Myles drawled. "You're really cynical, aren't you?"

"Cynical or truthful, Myles?" she said.

"You've done well for yourself, Brina," he countered. "Your husband may have lost his bid to become mayor of Philadelphia, but he made out even better when the governor appointed him to fill a vacant U.S. senate seat."

She swallowed a portion of the spinach and feta cheese omelet. "That was Thomas's ambition, not mine."

Myles took a sip of orange juice. "Please answer one question for me, Brina?"

"What is it?"

"If you disliked politics so much, then why did you marry a politician?"

Zabrina sighed audibly as she recalled her carefully re-hearsed script as to why she'd broken their engagement to marry Thomas Cooper. "I was in awe of Thomas Cooper, and I suppose him being twenty years my senior made him even more intriguing. He asked Daddy if he could marry me just weeks before you proposed."

"Were you sleeping with him?"

"No, Myles. I've never been one to sleep with more than one man."

How virtuous of you, Myles mused. "What did your father tell him?"

"He told Thomas he couldn't tell me who to marry."

Myles glared at her. "You accepted my proposal, while you were thinking of marrying another man."

Zabrina felt the heat of his gaze as she stared at her plate. She couldn't look at Myles or she would be forced to blurt out the truth. "When I spoke to my father he told me to follow my conscience."

"And what did your conscience tell you?"

"It told me to marry Thomas."

"It told you to marry Thomas," Myles mimicked. He sobered quickly. "Thomas Cooper took the woman who was to become *my* wife and claimed the son that should've been ours because you followed your conscience. If I'd followed my conscience, then I would hate you for your deception. But I don't hate you, Zabrina, because then I wouldn't have been able to move on with my life."

"Have you moved on, Myles?"

"Yes. I'm seriously considering buying a house."

Her eyebrows lifted. "You're buying a house in Philly?"

"No, Brina. I'm looking for one in Pittsburgh."

He'd moved on with his life, while Zabrina didn't know what she wanted to do with hers. And it hadn't dawned on her until now that Myles could possibly have a woman in Pittsburgh waiting for him to return at the end of the summer.

There had been a time when Myles was considered one of Philadelphia's most eligible bachelors, and she'd been too enamored of him to notice that other women flirted shamelessly with him. And why shouldn't she when, as a teenager, she'd done exactly that—flirted shamelessly with him.

They ate their breakfast in silence, each lost in their personal thoughts. Zabrina wished it'd been different, that she could've been matron of honor and Myles best man for Belinda and Griffin's wedding, that her son was Adam Eaton not Cooper, that every night she would go to sleep and every morning wake up beside Myles. She wanted to give Adam the brother or sister he always talked about.

But it was not to be, because she'd played the sacrifi-

cial lamb for her father in order to keep him from going to
prison. She didn't regret what she'd done and would do it
again if faced with the same predicament.

Thomas Cooper's promise that their marriage was in
name only and the fact that she'd had Myles Eaton's son
made her sacrifice more than worthwhile. Her father was
gone, Thomas was gone and Myles was no longer in her life.
Unwittingly, he'd given her a gift she would cherish forever.

Myles followed closely behind Zabrina's car during the
drive to Philadelphia. Although she'd said she was no
longer feeling the effects of the alcohol she'd consumed
the night before, he wanted to make certain she arrived
home without a mishap.

He was surprised when she maneuvered into an enclave
of recently constructed one-family homes less than a
quarter of a mile from where Belinda had purchased her
house. With him living in Belinda's house for the summer,
he and Zabrina were within walking distance of each other.

She'd moved out of the mansion where generations of
Coopers had lived for a more modest lifestyle with her son.
An emotion came over him that he immediately recognized
as a newfound respect for Zabrina. When she'd ended their
engagement he'd conjured up dozens of reasons why she
didn't want to marry him: he had been too demanding, he
had convinced her to sleep with him when she hadn't been
ready, he had put pressure on her to become a mother when
she'd wanted to wait at least two years.

He'd blamed himself, until the news surfaced that
Zabrina Mixon had married Thomas Cooper in a private
ceremony. Then it had all made sense. Thomas had come
from a long line of African-American politicians in Phila-

delphia dating back to the 1890s. Cooper was handsome, eloquent, wealthy and twenty years her senior. He was also a close friend of Isaac Mixon, and Zabrina marrying Cooper would cement the relationship between the consummate politician and the masterful political strategist.

Shifting into Park, Myles sat staring out the windshield as Zabrina got out of her car and came over to his driver's-side window. He smiled. Even with her bare face and her hair brushed off her forehead and behind her ears, she was still ravishing.

Reaching into the open window, Zabrina rested a hand on Myles's wrist. "Thank you, Myles."

His gaze lowered, lingering on her full, sultry mouth. "For what?"

"For taking care of me last night."

"Think nothing of it. That's what friends are supposed to do. Take care of each other."

Her eyebrows lifted slightly. "Are we friends, Myles?"

"Yes," Myles said after a long pause. "If we weren't friends, then I would've had sex with you. And, because it didn't happen, that makes us friends."

Zabrina closed her eyes for several seconds. Myles *had* changed. In the past, whenever she'd mentioned them having sex he'd corrected her to say it wasn't sex but making love, then had gone on to explain the differences.

"How else can I thank you aside from saying thank you?"

Myles reached for his cell phone resting in a console between the seats of the Range Rover. "Give me your numbers and I'll call you."

"Call me for what?" she asked as a thread of suspicion crept into her voice.

"Perhaps we can get together to take in a movie or go out to dinner before I go back to Pittsburgh."

Zabrina forced a smile. She didn't want to start up with Myles again only to have him leave at the end of the summer. Ten years before, she'd left him, and now he would be the one to leave her.

"Okay." She gave him the phone number to her house and her cell. Then, on impulse, she leaned into the window and pressed a kiss to his jaw. "Thank you again."

Myles nodded, mildly surprised at Zabrina's display of affection. He sat motionless, watching as she walked to the entrance of her home, opened the door and closed it behind her. He still could see the image of her long, shapely legs in the stilettos.

His gaze shifted to the tiny phone in his hand. Common sense told him to delete Zabrina's numbers, but he'd never been rational when it came to her. From the moment he'd kissed her for the first time, to when they'd shared a bed for the first time, nothing between them had ever been sensible.

He ran his free hand over his face as if to wipe away the frustration and pain of the past ten years. Myles couldn't fathom why despite her deceit he still wanted her. Just when he was certain he was over Zabrina, she was back in his life, reminding him of the searing passion they'd shared.

And despite her heart-wrenching deception, he still wanted her.

Chapter 6

Myles clocked the distance it took for him to drive from Zabrina's house to his sister's. It took exactly three minutes door to door.

He parked his sport-utility vehicle in the driveway rather than in the two-car garage. It was Sunday and he would've usually shared dinner with his parents, but after last night's wedding reception he knew the elder Eatons wanted to either sleep in late or relax.

He still had to settle into the house where he planned to spend his summer. Belinda had given him a quick walk-through of the two-story white house framed with dark blue molding and matching shutters. He'd teased his sister, saying that if she'd known she would be moving to Paoli less than six months after renovating the second floor to accommodate the needs of two teenage girls she could've saved a great deal of money.

He got out of the SUV, retrieved his overnight and garment bags from the rear seat and made his way up the porch. Myles unlocked the front door and deactivated the security system. Leaving the garment bag on a chair in the entryway, he walked to the rear of the house to the laundry room to empty the contents of the overnight bag into the hamper. Belinda had given him a crash course on operating the digital washer and dryer, which meant he didn't have to send out his laundry.

Not having a house with a porch and not waking up to trees and a green lawn weren't the only reasons why he'd grown tired of living in an apartment. Myles had also grown tired of shopping every week because he lacked storage in his apartment. He preferred going to a supermarket warehouse several times a year to buy in bulk. His teaching schedule had increased from two to three constitutional law classes, and his free time was now at a premium—he didn't want to get into his car and go shopping on a weekly basis. He liked big-city living, but as he grew older he realized he preferred a slower pace.

He'd grown up with his parents and three sisters in a six-bedroom, four-bath farmhouse in a Philadelphia suburb. His mother was a stay-at-home mom, negotiating the many squabbles between her four rambunctious children, while their physician father treated his many patients in the office connected to the main house. He knew Dwight Eaton was disappointed that none of his children had elected to pursue a career in medicine, but he had supported them in whatever career paths they'd chosen.

Myles hadn't realized he wanted to become a lawyer until he joined his high school's debate team. His verbal skills and quick thinking made him a standout whenever they competed with other high schools. Once he entered college he was able to hone his skills in mock court trials.

Walking out of the laundry room, he checked the pantry, then the refrigerator. When he'd called to tell Belinda that he planned to spend the summer in Philadelphia she'd offered him her house. The furniture in his nieces' bedrooms had been moved to Griffin's house in Paoli, but Belinda hadn't taken any of the other furniture. His sister had restocked the refrigerator and pantry before his arrival, making moving in smooth and stress-free.

When Belinda had informed him that she was going to marry Griffin Rice, Myles hadn't wanted to believe that two of his sisters had fallen in love with brothers. But, when he rethought the relationships in his family, he realized his sister Donna had named one of her daughters for his girlfriend. When Donna and Grant's fraternal twin girls were born, Donna had named one Sabrina, using the traditional *S* instead of *Z*.

He'd just turned on the under-the-counter television when the doorbell rang. Myles walked out of the kitchen to the front door. When he opened it he found his youngest sister Chandra and his twin nieces grinning at him.

"Surprise!" they chorused.

Chandra held up a large white shopping bag. "I brought breakfast."

Myles opened the door wider, smiling. "Come in. I hate to ruin your surprise, but I already ate breakfast."

Sabrina went on tiptoe to kiss her uncle. "Gram and Gramps put a Do Not Disturb sign on their doorknob, so Aunt Chandra decided on a take-out breakfast."

Sabrina was the mirror image of Belinda at her age. Myles had always thought her a little too mature and serious for her age. Layla, on the other hand, was more laid-back, funky. Both wore braces to correct an overbite, but it was Layla who opted for colorful bands rather than the clear ones worn by her twin. The girls would celebrate their thirteenth birthday in the fall, and every time he saw them they appeared to have grown several inches.

"Who's watching the puppies?" he asked the girls.

Belinda had called him earlier that spring to tell him that Griffin had purchased two Yorkshire terriers for their nieces with the hope that it would make them more responsible. He was introduced to the two puppies for the first time when he drove to Paoli to reunite with his brother-in-law.

Layla shared a look with her sister. "Nigel and Cecil are with the lady who owns their mother."

Sabrina sniffled. "Aunt Lindy and Uncle Griff said we can't have them until they get back from their honeymoon."

Chandra registered her brother's what's-going-on look? "Mom and Dad's subdivision has a no-dogs rule and Griffin's mother and father are leaving for Martha's Vineyard tomorrow."

Myles stared at his youngest sister. Although she'd recently celebrated her thirtieth birthday she looked much younger. Chandra's normally gold-brown complexion was several shades darker from the hot tropical sun. She'd spent more than two years in Central America as a Peace Corps volunteer. Chandra had taken a leave from her teaching position at a private elementary school to teach in Belize. She was also much thinner than she'd been in years. Either she wasn't eating enough or she was working much too hard.

"They can stay here with me," Myles volunteered, "that way you can come over and play with them." Ear-piercing shrieks filled the air as Layla and Sabrina jumped up and down, hugging each other.

"Thank you, Uncle Myles," they said in unison.

He tugged gently on the hair Layla had secured with an elastic band. "You're very welcome. After you guys eat breakfast, we'll drive over to Paoli to pick up your puppies."

Chandra handed Sabrina the bag. "Please take this into the kitchen. I need to speak to your uncle for a few minutes."

"Are you going to talk about grown folks business?" Layla asked.

"Yes, Miss Know-It-All," Chandra teased.

"Do we have to wait for you before we can eat, Aunt Chandra?" Sabrina asked.

Chandra shook her head. "No. You can eat without me." They sprinted toward the rear of the house. She realized it had to cost Griffin and Belinda a small fortune to feed growing teenagers.

Reaching for his sister's hand, Myles led her out to the porch. "What's up?"

Leaning against a thick column on the porch, Chandra folded her arms under her breasts. "Where did you disappear to last night?"

He narrowed his gaze. "It's been a very long time since I've had to account for my whereabouts, *little sister.*"

Chandra stared at her bare toes in a pair of leather sandals. "That came out all wrong."

"I'd say it did," Myles drawled.

A slight frown furrowed her smooth forehead. "I'm only asking because you disappeared at the same time Zabrina did, and I thought maybe the two of you were together."

"And what if we were, Chandra?"

"Were you?"

There came a beat of silence as brother and sister stared at each other. "Yes. She had too much to drink, and I took her to my room so she could sleep it off."

Chandra closed her eyes while shaking her head. "Myles, you do realize what you're doing?"

"What are you talking about?"

"Why are you starting up with her again? If she left you once, then there's always the possibility that she'll leave you again."

"Who said I was starting up with her, Chandra? What did you expect me to do? There was no way I was going to let her get behind the wheel of a car when she was under the influence. Her son recently lost his father and grandfather. Did you expect me to stand by and let him lose his mother, too?"

"I can understand your concern, Myles. But Zabrina is not your responsibility."

"She was last night."

"What about this morning? What about tomorrow and the next day and the day after that?" Chandra stopped her rant long enough to study her brother's impassive expression. "You're still not over her, are you?"

Myles, swallowing the biting words poised on the tip of his tongue, struggled not to lose his temper. When Zabrina had ended their engagement all of the Eatons were upset with the news. But twenty-year-old Chandra had appeared almost indifferent to the calamity as everyone scrambled to call out-of-town friends and relatives to inform them the wedding had been canceled. Apparently it'd taken a decade for Chandra's resentment of Zabrina to fester before coming to the surface.

"Let it go, Chandra." His voice, although soft, was cutting and lethal.

"But, how can you—"

"I said to let it go," he repeated. "What goes on between Brina and I has nothing to do with you."

She rolled her eyes. "If that's the way you want it."

Myles shot her a warning glare. "That's exactly how I want it." Turning on his heel, he opened the door and went inside the house, leaving his sister staring in his wake.

Chandra exhaled a breath. She didn't want to fight with her brother. As it was they rarely saw each other since she'd joined the Peace Corps, and she couldn't remember the last time Myles had spoken so harshly to her.

Myles was the perfect older brother, because he'd always protected his younger sisters. Once Myles reached adolescence his father had told him that it'd become his responsibility to take care of the women in the house, and that included his mother. She'd believed it had something to do with their father juggling his schedule when he was on call at the hospital while running his medical practice. Dr. Eaton had become an anomaly as one of a few general practitioners to still make house calls.

Unfortunately there was no one to protect Myles from Zabrina Mixon's treachery. Donna and Belinda were more vociferous in expressing their rage. But Chandra hadn't said anything because it'd been the only time in her life when she'd seriously considered giving someone a serious beat-down. By the time she'd returned home from New York, where she'd been enrolled at Columbia University, her anger had subsided.

Myles wanted her to let it go, and she would. She only had another three days before she returned to Belize, and she didn't want to spend the time she had left in the States arguing with her brother.

Leaning away from the column, she walked off the porch and into the house.

Zabrina sat on a cushioned rocker on her porch, watching as dusk descended over the landscape like someone slowly pulling down a shade. She'd prepared a light dinner, watched the evening news, then settled down to read. But restlessness, akin to an itch she couldn't scratch, assailed her and she gave up trying to read to sit on the porch.

She hadn't wanted to admit it, but she missed her son. She'd agreed to let Adam spend a month with his great-aunt and younger cousins. Zabrina had wrestled with her conscience when her cousin had asked Adam to spend time with her young children, and in the end had relented.

Her son was bright, curious and amazingly artistic, and she'd found it a daily struggle not to become an overly protective mother. Permitting Adam to spend time with his cousins was the first step.

Resting her bare feet on a cushioned footstool, she closed her eyes and inhaled the scent of blooming night flowers. The gentle peace she hadn't felt in years swept over Zabrina. Her three-bedroom, two-bath house was much smaller than the twelve-bedroom mausoleum she'd lived in with Thomas, but it was hers and hers alone. Once she decided to sell the house that had been home to generations of Coopers she knew she'd taken the first step to empower herself.

Thomas's attorney had encouraged her to hold on to the house and property for investment purposes. What he didn't understand was that she hated living in a place that

made her feel as if she were in a museum. She'd had someone from an auction house appraise the house's contents,
and was shocked with the final accounting.

"What's up, Zabrina?"

She opened her eyes and sat up straighter, hearing her
closest neighbor's greeting. The day she and Adam moved
in, Rachel Copeland had come over with her eight-year-
old daughter and eleven-year-old son to introduce her
family and bring her a pan of lasagna. Rachel confided that
she'd been praying for someone with a child to purchase
the newly constructed home so her children would have
someone to play with. Most of the homeowners in the two-
or three-bedroom subdivision were either young childless
couples or retired couples looking to downsize.

She and Rachel had one thing in common—both were
widows. Rachel had lost her military career-officer husband in Afghanistan. Although Zabrina told her that she'd
lost her husband in a drowning accident, she'd neglected
to tell her that her late husband had been Pennsylvania's
junior senator. She'd managed to keep to herself while
settling in. A bus came to pick up Adam to take him to a
private school and brought him back in the afternoon.

Zabrina waved to her neighbor. "Not much, Rachel."

Rachel walked up the porch steps and folded her tall,
slender body down into a dark green wicker chair with a
green-and-white-striped cushion. "The weather is really
nice tonight."

Zabrina smiled at her neighbor. Rachel's pale blond
hair was pulled off her thin face into a ponytail. She
would've been thought of as plain if not for her large eyes
that were more violet than blue. Her nose was straight, thin
and her lower lip full enough to make her appear petulant.

Rachel revealed that she'd been a catalogue model before she married her late husband.

"It's perfect." A ceiling fan stirred the warm gentle breeze.

Rachel let out an audible sigh. "I don't know why I hadn't thought of putting in a ceiling fan on my porch."

"I almost regretted having it installed when I caught Adam poking at it with a tree branch. There were splinters everywhere. Once I made certain he was not injured, I grounded him for a week. And that meant no drawing."

"No drawing or no television?"

"For my son it's no drawing. He says he wants to be an animator when he grows up."

Rachel's pale eyebrows shot up. "He likes drawing that much?"

Zabrina nodded. "Yes. It's become an obsession with him. I've tried to get him involved in other things, but he quickly loses interest."

"My Maggie is a dance fanatic and Shane believes he's a kung fu master. I spend all of my free time chauffeuring them between dance and karate classes. My mother came over earlier and took them home with her. Now that they're on summer break I'll have a little more time for myself." Rachel sat up straighter. "What do you say we go out clubbing one night next week?"

Zabrina gave her an incredulous look. "You're kidding, aren't you?"

Rachel leaned forward. "Do I look like I'm kidding? My husband's been dead three years and he had long talks about what he wanted for me if he didn't come back alive. He told me that he didn't want me to spend the rest of my life mourning for him, and now I realize what he was trying to tell me. I'm thirty-four years old and I'm lonely *and* horny. Even if I don't sleep with a man I want one to hold me close and tell me things a woman wants and needs to hear."

Zabrina smiled. "Well, if you put it that way, then I'll go out with you."

She wanted to tell her neighbor that she hadn't been out clubbing but had gone to a wedding where she'd flirted with a man she had no intention of seeing again, and she'd drunk too much to forget another whom she'd never stopped loving.

Rachel's smile was dazzling. "Thanks." She pushed to her feet. "I don't know about you, but I'd like to go for a walk."

Zabrina swung her legs over the footstool and stood up. "Let me get my shoes and I'll join you."

Zabrina was glad Rachel had suggested going for a walk. It was just what she needed to shake off a case of doldrums, and she'd quickly discovered they weren't the only ones who were out for a walk. Couples—young and some not so young—strolled along a lit path that bordered a bird sanctuary. There were joggers and others walking dogs.

She and Rachel talked about everything from recipes to the economy and their children. What they did not talk about were men, or the lack of men in their lives. Zabrina understood Rachel's need to meet a man. After all, she'd had more than three years to mourn the death of her husband and the father of her children, while her own arranged marriage had ended less than a year ago.

Reaching for Rachel's arm, Zabrina pulled her away from two frisky puppies heading for her. "Watch out."

Rachel shook off her hand, bending down to touch the tiny bundles of fur. "Aren't you two just too cute?"

Zabrina glanced up at the man pulling gently on the leashes of the yapping Yorkshire terriers. "Myles?"

Myles nodded. "Good evening, Brina."

"What…what are you doing around here?"

Myles's gaze swept over the woman who unknowingly still held a piece of his heart. "I'm staying at Belinda's house."

Her eyelids fluttering, Zabrina tried to process what Myles had just told her. "But, she told me she was moving to Paoli." A small town north of Philadelphia, Paoli was a friendly close-knit community of fifty-four hundred that was family-oriented.

"She did, but with the housing market the way it is she's decided to hold on to her house until the market improves."

Zabrina hadn't realized how fast her heart was beating until she felt the rapid pulse in her lip. Myles was going to spend the summer in a house within walking distance of her own. Each time she walked or drove along the road near the bird sanctuary she knew she would always look for a glimpse of Myles Eaton.

She pointed to the puppies that were now yapping at Rachel. "Do they belong to you?"

"No! Do I look like the lap-dog type?"

"Easy, Myles," Zabrina said, biting back a smile. She knew she'd hit a raw nerve because she was aware that he liked big dogs.

"They belong to my nieces."

She hunkered down, rubbing one of the pups behind the ears. "You are so cute. What's your name, baby?"

Myles stared at Zabrina kneeling on the ground in front of him, curbing the urge to run his fingers through her hair. He recalled the number of times he'd wakened to find her long hair spread over the pillow beside his. Those were days and nights he'd believed would never end.

"I think that one is Cecil, and the other is Nigel."

Zabrina came to her feet. "They are adorable. Please excuse me, but I'm forgetting my manners. Myles, this is my neighbor Rachel Copeland. Rachel, Myles Eaton."

Rachel offered Myles her hand. "It's very nice meeting you. How long have you and Zabrina known each other?"

Myles stared at Zabrina. "We grew up together."

"Zabrina and I are going clubbing in a few days. Would you like to come with us?" Rachel asked. She wasn't smiling, but grinning. "You can bring your wife or girlfriend along if you want."

"Rachel!"

Zabrina couldn't understand what had gotten into her neighbor. First she'd talked about being horny, and now she'd invited a stranger to go out with them, as well as Myles's wife or girlfriend, though Zabrina doubted he had one. If he'd had a wife there was no doubt she would've come with him to her sister-in-law's wedding, and if there was a serious girlfriend, then she, too, would've attended the wedding.

Rachel turned and glared at Zabrina in disbelief. It was apparent Myles and Zabrina hadn't seen each other in a while or else she would've known he lived within walking distance of their subdivision. And inviting him to go out with them, even if he was involved with someone, would be the perfect cover for them not to look like two desperate women trolling clubs to pick up men.

"It's obvious you and Myles haven't seen each other in a while, so I thought inviting him along would give you two the opportunity to reminisce."

Myles smiled when Zabrina stared at the ground. He knew she was uneasy about interacting with him, because what they'd shared the night before wasn't easily forgotten.

"Rachel's right," he said quietly. "Hanging out together will allow us to talk about old times. Where and when are you going?"

Rachel spoke first. "We're not certain. But it will be this week." She pulled a tiny cell phone from the pocket of her shorts. "Give me your number and I'll call and let you know."

Myles noticed the narrow gold band on the ring finger of the chatty blonde's right hand. His gaze shifted to Zabrina's bare fingers, then her wide-eyed stare. "I have Zabrina's numbers," he said, after a long pause.

Rachel clapped her hands. "That's great! You can call her and she'll let you know what's up after we decide on a place...unless you can recommend one."

"I'll let Brina know." Myles didn't want to commit until he spoke to a former high-school classmate. Hugh Ormond had changed careers, going from investment banker to chef and eventually opening an upscale restaurant that featured dining and dancing a block from Broad Street, affectionately known to Philadelphians as Avenue of the Arts.

Rachel extended her hand for the second time. "Again, it's a pleasure to meet you, Myles."

He smiled the sexy smile that never failed to make a woman take pause. "The pleasure is all mine, Rachel."

Zabrina's neighbor had provided him with the perfect excuse to see her again.

"I guess we'll see you soon," Rachel crooned.

Myles's smile grew wider. "That you will." He nodded to Zabrina. "Good night, Brina."

She returned a smile that failed to reach her eyes. "Good

night, Myles." She bent over to pat the Yorkies. They jumped up in an attempt to lick her face, but she pulled back in time.

Taking Rachel's arm, she forcibly pulled her to retrace their route. "I could kill you for inviting Myles to go out with us," she hissed between her teeth, although they were far enough away from Myles so that he wouldn't hear her rant. "You made it seem as if we're desperate, widows gone wild."

Rachel extricated her arm. "What are you talking about?"

"What if I didn't want him to go out with us?"

"Why wouldn't you, Zabrina? Didn't the two of you grow up together?"

"I was friends with one of his sisters."

"Is he married, Zabrina?"

"No."

"Does he have a special woman?"

"I don't know," Zabrina answered truthfully.

Rachel flashed a knowing smile. "We'll find out soon enough when we all go out together."

Zabrina stopped mid-stride. "Why your sudden interest in Myles Eaton?"

Resting her hands on her slim hips, Rachel pushed her face close to Zabrina's. "I'm not interested in him for myself, but for you. You were so busy playing with the puppies that you couldn't see the lust in Myles's eyes. And if I didn't know better I'd think you have something wrong with your eyes if you didn't notice that he's so hot he sizzles."

"If he's so hot, then why don't you go after him?"

"Maybe I will once I find out whether he's available. That is, *if* you don't want him."

Rachel's pronouncement rendered Zabrina speechless

and motionless. She'd seen a photograph of her neighbor's late husband, and he was the complete opposite of Myles. But who was she to say what Rachel's type was? She didn't want to admit that she was jealous. For years she'd thought of Myles as hers even though she'd married another man. Every night when she went to bed—alone—she pretended Myles Eaton was in bed with her. And there were times when she prayed he wouldn't find another woman to love because that meant losing him forever. Myles had always said that when he married it would be for the rest of his life.

The sky had darkened and millions of stars twinkled in the heavens when Zabrina and Rachel returned home. She said good-night to Rachel, walked up the porch to her house and unlocked the door. Silence greeted her as she walked in. It wasn't often the house was silent because either a radio or the television provided background noise while she cooked or completed her household chores.

After Adam came home from school he went through the ritual of washing his hands and changing out of his school uniform before settling down at the kitchen table to do his homework. By the time he finished dinner was ready. It was their time together when Adam recounted what had gone on in his classes.

Although Adam looked nothing like Myles, his facial expressions and body language were almost identical to his biological father's. Zabrina dreaded the time when she would have to tell her son the truth about the man who'd fathered him.

She dreaded it almost as much as the revelation that the grandfather he'd loved and respected was a thief.

Chapter 7

Zabrina had just finished applying her makeup when the doorbell chimed. The contrast of the smoky shadow on her eyelids made her eyes appear lighter than they actually were.

As promised, Myles had called her Monday evening to inform her that he'd made dinner reservations for three at a popular restaurant in the heart of downtown Philadelphia that featured live music and dancing. His mention of reservations for three answered her question as to whether he would have a fourth person join them. If she hadn't lived a cloistered existence for the past decade, Zabrina would've invited a man to come along as her date in order to put some physical distance between herself and Myles, because it would take a miracle for her to exorcise him from her heart. He was the first man with whom she'd fallen in love, and she would love him forever.

Walking out of the en suite bathroom through the

bedroom, she made her way down the carpeted hallway to the staircase in a pair of four-inch black crepe satin Christian Louboutin pumps with an asymmetric bow. She'd selected the designer footwear for Thomas's swearing-in ceremony, but hadn't attended because she'd come down with pneumonia and her doctor had advised against traveling to D.C.

What was ironic was that her closets were filled with designer clothes and shoes she'd never worn, shoes and clothes purchased for her by the young man whose responsibility it was to dress his boss and his boss's wife. Most times the designer garments remained on the padded hangers when she refused to attend a dinner party or fundraiser with Thomas. He had lost his temper several times, but when she threatened to divulge that he'd blackmailed her into marrying him he glared at her and stalked out of her bedroom suite. It was the last time he'd asked her to accompany him. However, her wardrobe continued to increase with Thomas's hope that she would eventually change her mind.

She never did.

When she'd taken the shoes out of the box, Zabrina glanced at the price tag for the first time. Spending nine hundred dollars for a pair of shoes was unconscionable, and there were at least four-dozen boxes containing shoes comparable to the pair she'd selected to go out with Myles and Rachel. Slim black stretch cuffed slacks and a white long-sleeved cotton wrapped-waist blouse completed her casual chic outfit.

Glancing through the side window in the door, she saw Myles's SUV parked in her driveway. She opened the door and went completely still as a sensual smile spread across

Myles's face. The gesture made her feel something she'd almost forgotten existed. Even when she woke Sunday morning to discover that she was sharing the same bed as Myles Eaton, none of the sensations now coursing through her body had been evident. Maybe it was because her senses had been dulled by alcohol, but the tiny tremors between her legs made it difficult for her to maintain her balance in the high heels.

"You're early." He'd come half an hour before he was supposed to pick her up. She opened the door wider, and he walked into the expansive foyer that led to the living room. She closed the door, turned around pressing her back to the door.

Myles registered the husky quality of her voice. His smile slipped slowly away when he stared at Zabrina under the soft, flattering glow from a chandelier hanging overhead. Unconsciously Zabrina was seducing him with her smoky voice and sparkling eyes. His gaze lingered on her face. Her luminous eyes, the exotic slant of high cheekbones and her full lush mouth were sexually arousing. She was thinner than she'd been when they were engaged, but her size did not diminish her femininity. There was enough roundness in her hips to belie any notion of her being mistaken for a boy.

Leaning closer, he kissed her cheek. "How did you get so tall?"

Zabrina laughed softly. "It's the heels." Extending her foot, she displayed the stilettos.

His eyebrows lifted. The heels she wore were higher than the ones she'd had on at Belinda's wedding. "Are you certain you'll be able to dance in those?"

Zabrina affected a sensual pout, drawing Myles's gaze

to lips enhanced by a glossy magenta. The shade was perfect for her lightly tanned face. "I'll sit out the fast tunes." His eyelids lowered, reminding Zabrina of a predator watching and waiting for the exact moment to seize its intended prey. "Should I add your name to my dance card?"

If you think I'm taking you out so you can dance and flirt with other men, then you've truly lost your mind.

The thought had popped into and out of Myles's head in the blink of an eye. In that instant he had to admit that Chandra was right. Just when he'd believed he'd gotten over Zabrina, she'd come back into his life. Even if he'd been able to exorcise her from his thoughts, what he hadn't been able to forget was the searing heat and passion between them.

The first time he and Zabrina had shared a bed he'd known she was different—special. And it hadn't had anything to do with her being a virgin. There was a time when Myles thought he'd remained faithful to his sister's best friend because he'd taken her innocence. But, when he compared her to the other women he'd slept with, he knew her virginity did not figure into the equation. The reality was that he had fallen in love with Zabrina before they'd slept together.

She could always get him to laugh even when he hadn't felt like laughing. She wasn't as needy as some of the women he'd known. They were the ones who complained if he didn't call them every day, or tell them they were pretty. Not only was Zabrina beautiful, but she was also smart and independent—something he hadn't expected her to be since she'd grown up pampered by her father.

He hadn't remembered Zabrina's mother that well. He'd

been twelve when she'd finally lost her mother to brain cancer. At that age he'd begun noticing girls and sports had become a priority. However, he wasn't completely oblivious to the gossip about Jacinta Mixon's shadowy background. Some said that the beautiful woman was the product of a short-lived marriage between an African-American soldier and a young woman he'd met in the Philippines. Others claimed that she'd come from Mexico with her migrant farming family and caught the eye of Isaac Mixon when he was stationed at Fort Sam Houston in Texas. Whatever her racial or ethnic background, Jacinta had given Isaac an incredible child.

Myles blinked as if coming out of a trance. "What do you think, Brina?" he asked after a long silence.

A slight frown appeared between Zabrina's eyes. Myles was looking at her as if she were a complete stranger. "I don't know what to think. That's why I asked, Myles."

"Of course I want to dance with you."

She smiled. "Good. I just have to comb my hair, then I'll be ready." She'd washed her hair, applied a small amount of gel and all she had to do was style it.

"Do you mind if I look around your house?"

Myles's question threw Zabrina for a few seconds. "No, I don't mind. Why don't you come upstairs with me, then you can work your way down."

"I'm trying to get an idea of what kind of house I want to buy."

Turning on her heels, Zabrina walked to the staircase. "Whatever you choose should complement its surroundings," she said over her shoulder as she climbed the stairs. Myles was right behind her.

"There are a few new developments going up in some

of Pittsburgh's suburbs, but what I don't want is a cookie-cutter house."

"Why don't you have it built to your specifications?"

Myles stared at the gentle sway of hips as Zabrina made her way along the carpeted hallway. "I don't want to wait that long. I have a lease on an apartment that's due to expire at the end of August. I'd like to move into a house before Labor Day. I've been preapproved, so all I have to do is find the house I want."

Zabrina stopped at her bedroom. "I'm going to be in here. The bathroom is across the hall, my son's room is on the left and a guest bedroom is at the end of the hall on the right."

Myles stared at the woman whose head was only several inches below his. Zabrina stood close to six feet in her heels. "How many bathrooms do you have?"

"There are two full baths upstairs and one half bath off the kitchen."

"Your house looks bigger than Belinda's."

"It is. Her subdivision is ten years older than this one. The same developer designed both subdivisions. But when he decided to build here, putting up McMansions was all the rage. These homes are what I call mini-McMansions. The smaller ones range between twenty-five hundred and three thousand square feet. The larger ones go as high as five thousand square feet."

"I doubt if I'll need five thousand square feet. Three or four would be more than enough. What I really want is a wraparound porch, lots of trees and enough property that a couple of dogs can have the run of the place."

Zabrina patted his arm.

"It sounds as if you're nostalgic for your childhood home."

A beat passed as Myles thought about what Zabrina had

said. She was right. He *was* nostalgic, longing for what was and would never be again. "Maybe I am," he admitted reluctantly. "What about you, Brina?"

"What about me?"

"You've spent the past decade living in a mansion with a staff to see to your every need, and you gave it all up to live here?"

Her delicate jaw hardened. "That house wasn't mine. It belonged to Thomas. As his widow I could do whatever I wanted with it, and I decided to sell it."

"What about your son, Brina? He's a Cooper. Shouldn't he live in his family's home? After all, the house was his birthright."

Thomas Cooper came from a prominent Philadelphia African-American family. Ephraim Cooper had been accused of being a front man for a group of unscrupulous businessmen when he sold worthless railroad stock to poor blacks who wanted to cash in on the American dream.

Ephraim, a self-taught attorney, successfully defended himself in court, suing the men he worked for. He won the case and earned a reputation as a champion of the underdog. The publicity made him one of the most sought-after attorneys in Philadelphia. He enlarged his practice, built what came to be known as Cooper Hall and eventually returned all of the monies to those who'd invested in the phony railroad stock scheme. Before Ephraim passed away he'd been referred to as the unofficial mayor of Philadelphia's Negro population.

Zabrina closed her eyes and swallowed hard in an attempt to suppress the rage threatening to erupt. When she opened her eyes all traces of gold were missing, leaving them a cold, frosty green.

"Do not talk to me about something you know nothing about. What I did was sell what you think was my son's so-called birthright and put the proceeds in an account for his future. His education and the man that he will become mean more to me than his living in a museum with servants waiting on him hand and foot."

Myles realized he'd pushed the wrong button when he'd mentioned her son. It was apparent discussing Adam Cooper was taboo. It was a mistake he would not repeat. "You're right. I'm sorry," he said, apologizing.

Zabrina nodded. "I'm sorry I went off on you, Myles. I suppose I'm a little protective when it comes to Adam."

He winked at her. "I guess being protective comes with parenthood. Now that I've taken my foot out of my mouth I'm going to see the rest of your house."

Myles walked to the end of the hall, peered into the guest bedroom and flipped the wall switch. The space was twice the size of his Pittsburgh bedroom. Zabrina had decorated it in a soft, calming taupe and seafoam green. The room held a queen-size bed, double dresser and nightstands, and a love seat covered in soft green was positioned under a trio of windows. Sheers were hung above the windows, a rug in a muted color, a stack of books and magazines on a low table beside the love seat and the ceiling fan overhead created a calm, relaxed feel to the room.

Turning off the light, he moved down the hall to the bathroom: recessed lights, white mosaic tile, a garden tub with a Jacuzzi, twin stainless-steel sinks, a free-standing shower and a dressing area with mirrored walls made the space appear twice as large.

Adam's room was the quintessential boy's bedroom with a trundle bed covered with a red, white and blue patchwork quilt. The colors were repeated in the rug and built-in shelves cradling books, a desktop computer, printer and television. The bedroom was spotless.

Myles's mouth twitched in amusement when he remembered Roberta Eaton's reaction whenever she opened the door to his third-story bedroom. Because he was the only boy, he'd been given the attic bedroom. She usually had to scour the room to find mismatched socks under the bed, underwear, T-shirts and occasionally dress slacks on the floor of the closets in order to put them in the wash or send them to the dry cleaner. It was only when he moved into his own condo that he took steps to keep his living quarters neat *and* clean. He hired a cleaning service. He walked over to Zabrina's bedroom, rapping lightly on the door.

"Come in," Zabrina called out from somewhere behind the door.

Myles entered the master bedroom, stopping when he saw the elaborately carved mahogany four-poster bed with all-white bed linens that was the room's focal point. The mahogany furniture and creamy white fabrics harkened back to a bygone era where women sipped tea on the veranda.

"Where are you, Brina?"

"I'm in the bathroom."

He turned in the direction of her voice and stood at the entrance to her bathroom. It wasn't a bathroom so much as it was a home spa. A cedar soaking tub, candles and incense, a built-in bench lined with pillows for lounging or meditating offered a comfortable spot to stretch out before or after soaking or sitting in the sauna. The windows were covered with shades that let light in while providing complete privacy.

Zabrina sat at a dressing table putting the finishing

touches on her hair. Using her fingers, she'd lifted the damp strands at the crown and feathered wisps over her forehead.

Myles entered the bathroom. "Did all of this come with the house?"

Smiling at his reflection in the mirror, Zabrina shook her head. "Unfortunately, it didn't. I had to sleep in the guest bedroom for three weeks while the contractor completed the renovations. I was vacuuming up dust for at least a month."

He took another step, bringing him closer to where she sat. "It's incredible."

"If you ever want to come over and unwind in the sauna, just let me know. Spending half an hour in the steam shower, then soaking in the tub is the cure for whatever ails you."

Myles pushed his hands into the pockets of his suit trousers. "As much as I'd like to take you up on your offer, I can't do that, Brina."

Gazing into his dark eyes in the mirror, Zabrina frowned slightly. "Why can't you?"

"What would your son think if he saw a strange man lounging in his mother's bathroom?"

Zabrina came to her feet, her gaze meeting and fusing with Myles's. "Do you think I would invite you to come over when my son is here?"

"You tell me, Brina."

"The answer is no, Myles. Adam has never seen me with any other man except for Thomas. And if he were to see one in my bedroom then it would be my husband."

Raising his right hand, Myles ran the back of it over her cheek. "Would you ever get married again?"

Zabrina closed her eyes rather than look at the tenderness in Myles's eyes. "I would if he were the right man."

He frowned. "What do you mean by the right man?"

She opened her eyes. "He would have to be a good father and role model for Adam."

"What about you, Brina? What would you want for yourself?" Myles asked.

Brina said the first thing that came to mind. "Sex."

Myles lowered his head, unable to believe what he'd just heard. "You're kidding, aren't you?"

"Do I look like I'm kidding?"

Zabrina hadn't lied to Myles. It had been more than a decade since she'd been made love to. Unlike Rachel, who admitted to being horny, she had been too ashamed to openly admit it until now. Ten years was a long time to deny her own needs or the strong yearnings that unexpectedly swept over her. Surprised by her admission, Myles stared at her in disbelief.

"Why are you looking at me like that? Would it be less shocking if the roles were reversed, and you were the one saying that you wanted to have sex with me?"

"Is that what you want from me?" he asked, recovering his composure.

"Sure, but only if you're up for it," she countered. "It would just be for the summer."

"What about Adam?"

"What about him, Myles?"

"You can't expect me to sleep with you while he's in the house."

Zabrina was hard-pressed not to laugh. For the first time in years she felt empowered, dictating what she wanted or didn't want to do with every phase of her life. Although she'd refused to pretend to be the dutiful wife when Thomas wanted her to accompany him, legally she'd been his wife. Even after her father had passed away, Zabrina still hadn't been willing to divorce Thomas. As long as he didn't try to exercise his conjugal rights or interfere with her relationship with Adam she'd continued to play out the charade.

"We can sleep together at your place whenever Adam stays with his relatives or has a sleepover with his friends."

"What happens at the end of the summer, Zabrina?"

Myles was still trying to grasp the enormity of her unusual suggestion. This was a Zabrina he truly didn't know. When it came to women he'd always been the one doing the propositioning and usually not the other way around. This was not to say that women hadn't let him know they were interested in more than a platonic liaison, but they'd never been as candid as Zabrina.

"We go our separate ways to live our separate lives."

Damn, he mused. When had she become so insensitive? "Why me, Brina?" he asked. "Why not choose some other man to be your sex toy?"

"Why not you, Myles?" she said, answering his question with another question. "We have a history. And if people see us together they'll think we're just old friends hanging out together for the summer."

"Friends who were once engaged," Myles reminded her.

"That, too," she countered. "There are a lot of couples who were either married or break up and are still friends."

Her initial bravado fading quickly, Zabrina chided herself for broaching the subject of sleeping with Myles. Her ego and vanity had surpassed common sense. She tilted her chin in a haughty gesture. "Forget I mentioned it."

Reaching out, Myles pulled Zabrina close to his chest. A mysterious glow fired the raven orbs staring back at her. "I can't forget it any more than I can forget what we had, or what we once meant to each other. If you want a sex partner for the summer, then I'll oblige you. And don't concern yourself with birth control, because I'll assume responsibility for using protection."

Pinpoints of heat flamed in her face. She'd just propositioned her former fiancé, and he'd accepted. At thirty-three she'd become not only reckless, but shameless. Sleeping with Myles meant she didn't have to troll the clubs or the Internet looking for a man.

"Thank you." It was apparent he'd remembered the number of times she'd had to change contraceptives because of the side effects.

"You're welcome," Myles whispered, seconds before he sealed their arrangement with a searing kiss that weakened her knees. Nothing had changed. It was as if a day rather than a decade had passed between them. Her arms came up, she pressing closer as she wound her arms around his neck, while reveling in the taste and feel of his mouth on hers.

Zabrina clung to Myles as if she depended on him for her next breath. She loved him. She missed him and the passion he elicited with a single glance. Her fingers grazed the nape of his neck. Zabrina wanted Myles, wanted to strip him naked and lie between his legs until he assuaged her pent-up sexual frustration.

The doorbell rang for the second time, and she went completely still. "That's Rachel," she whispered against Myles's parted lips.

Cradling her face between his hands, Myles winked at Zabrina. "Send her away."

With wide eyes, she said, "I can't. Rachel has been really looking forward to going out tonight."

His eyebrows lifted as he brushed his mouth over hers.

"What about you, Brina? Are you looking forward to going out, too?"

"Yes, I am," she said truthfully.

"Okay. To be continued."

"To be continued," she repeated. Hand-in-hand, they walked out of the bedroom and down the staircase. Zabrina reached for her small leather purse while Myles opened the door.

Rachel Copeland had morphed from a suburban house-wife into a seductive siren. Her blond hair was a mass of tiny curls, and a body-hugging tank dress and matching strappy black sandals had replaced her ubiquitous T-shirt and jeans. Despite having given birth to two children there was no doubt she still could get modeling assignments.

Zabrina gasped. Rachel was certain to turn heads with her revealing outfit. "You look incredible, Rachel."

Rachel tossed her head and her flaxen curls bounced as if they'd taken on a life of their own. She looked every inch the model with her expertly made-up face. "Thank you. And, you're one hot-looking widow!"

Zabrina winced. Rachel was the widow of a war hero, and she saw herself as a single mother. Glancing over her shoulder, she smiled at Myles. "We're ready when-ever you are."

He waited for Zabrina to punch in the code for the security system and lock the door. He escorted both women to where he'd parked his SUV. Opening the passenger-side door, he scooped up Zabrina and placed her on the leather seat, then helped Rachel into her seat. He'd doubted whether either of them would've been able to get into the vehicle unassisted because of their footwear.

Try as he could, Myles didn't understand why women

insisted on wearing such high heels. However, there was an upside to stilettos—they made a woman's legs look incredibly sexy.

After all, he was a leg man.

Chapter 8

Myles pocketed his valet stub, then escorted Rachel and Zabrina through the restaurant's parking lot to Whispers. The upscale supper club had a three-week wait for dinner reservations, but Myles had jumped to the head of the list because he and Hugh Ormond had played on the same high-school football team. They'd lost touch after graduating, but reconnected the year before at their twentieth high-school reunion.

A doorman opened the door for them, his gaze sweeping over the two women clinging to Myles's arm. "Welcome to Whispers. I hope you and *your ladies* have an enjoyable evening."

"*Are* we your ladies, Myles?" Zabrina teased, sotto voce. His response was to narrow his gaze.

"How on earth did you get a reservation to this place?" Rachel whispered to Myles.

"A friend owns it."

"I'm going to like hanging out with you and Zabrina." Rachel had read about the grand opening of the club in the entertainment section of the local newspaper. The food critic had given the cuisine, decor, ambience and live entertainment his highest rating.

Myles approached the hostess. "I have a reservation for three at seven."

The young woman smiled at Myles. "Your name, sir?"

"Eaton."

Her smile brightened when she signaled the maître d'. "Mr. Ormond wants you to let him know when the Eaton party arrives."

The dark-suited, slightly built, balding man bowed elegantly from the waist. "*Monsieur, mesdames.* Please follow me."

Zabrina shared a smile with Rachel. The establishment was intimate and aesthetically pleasing, confirming it was the ideal venue for a rendezvous. Tables with seating for two or four were positioned far enough away from other diners to insure privacy. If they'd been placed closer, the restaurant's seating capacity would have doubled.

Whoever had designed the restaurant had incorporated elements of feng shui. The interior had come alive with live plants, the soft sound of gurgling fountains and an enormous fish tank, filled with colorful exotic fish, that spanned the entire length of the wall.

They were shown to a table with seating for four near the band playing Latin music. Several couples were up on the dance floor, swaying to the seductive rhythm.

Myles pulled out a chair, seating Zabrina, while a waiter came over to seat Rachel. Myles glanced up when a shadow loomed over the table. Rising to his feet, he gave Hugh Ormond a rough embrace.

Hugh pounded his former schoolmate's back. "I'm glad you could make it." He took the empty chair as Myles made the introductions.

"Hugh, the lady to my left is Zabrina Cooper and the one on your right is Rachel Copeland. Ladies, Hugh Ormond, owner and executive chef of Whispers."

Zabrina and Rachel gave the obligatory greetings, both enthralled with the man who exuded charm effortlessly. Tall and solidly built with cropped sandy-brown hair and sparkling gray eyes, Hugh Ormond had a quick smile and a velvet voice. When he ordered a bottle of champagne for the table, Zabrina felt the heat from Myles's gaze on her face. She sat up straighter when his hand caressed the small of her back.

"Don't worry, baby. I promise not to take advantage of you if you have more than one glass," Myles whispered in her ear.

"I'm not worried, darling," she said softly. "I trust you."

The moment the endearment slipped from her lips Zabrina felt as if time stood still, as if the past ten years hadn't happened. A slow warming began in her chest and wove its way down her body and settled between her thighs.

She'd thought herself brazen when she'd told Myles that she wanted him to make love to her but realized she was being honest. It was the first time since before she'd called her fiancé to tell him that she was in love with another man that she was honest with him *and* with herself.

What Zabrina had tired of was: pretending she was a dutiful wife when she posed with Thomas and Adam for an official family photograph, pretending all was well whenever they were forced to share the same space, pretending to grieve the loss of her husband *and* pretending to be strong for her son when he had to deal with the loss of his grandfather and father within months of each other.

Adam loved Thomas, but adored his grandfather. Isaac was always there when Thomas hadn't been. And whenever his father was around, the young boy did everything possible to get Thomas's attention. Once Thomas was appointed to fill the vacant senate seat, spending more time in D.C. than he did in Philadelphia, Adam transferred his affection from his father to his grandfather.

In order to help her son cope with the loss of two important men in his life Zabrina had arranged for him to see a child psychologist, and what was revealed in those sessions had rocked Zabrina to her very core. Adam had said Thomas always made him feel like a dog as he patted his head whenever he told him he'd aced a test. It'd been Grandpa who took him to baseball and football games when his father was too busy. It'd been Grandpa who accompanied his mother to parent-teacher conferences and it'd been Grandpa who'd saved every one of his drawings and had them bound like the many books lining the mansion's bookshelves.

She was forthcoming when she accepted blame for the distance between father and son, because Thomas had never really wanted children. Zabrina didn't tell the psychologist that she'd been blackmailed into marrying Thomas Cooper, but knew eventually she would have to tell Adam the truth. She wanted to wait until he was old enough to understand the reason she had to protect his beloved grandfather.

"Are you all right, Brina?"

She blinked as if coming out of a trance. "Yes. Why?"

Myles gave Zabrina a long, penetrating stare. She appeared distracted, and he wondered if it was because they'd agreed to sleep together again. Cupping her elbow, he leaned closer. "Come dance with me."

"Now?"

"Yes, now."

Myles wanted to talk to Zabrina, but he didn't want Hugh or Rachel to overhear what he wanted to tell her. He stood up and then eased Zabrina to her feet. Wrapping an arm around her waist, he led her to the dance floor. Easing her into a close embrace, he molded her length to his.

"What's the matter, Brina?" He felt her stiffen with his query before she relaxed again.

"What makes you think something is the matter?"

"You're distracted, and I've never known you to daydream."

Zabrina closed her eyes. "That's because I've changed, Myles. I have a lot more responsibility now."

"That may be true, but it's more than that."

"What are you getting at, Myles?"

"Why did you really ask me to sleep with you?"

Zabrina knew she couldn't tell him that her husband had never consummated their marriage, so she said the next best thing. "I'm lonely, Myles. I've been lonely for a very long time."

Myles missed a step with Zabrina's admission, but recovered quickly. It was apparent her marriage to Thomas Cooper was far from ideal. But then, what had she expected from a politician? It was apparent her late husband had neglected her and she wanted Myles to make up for the loss of affection.

"I can't be a substitute for your late husband, Brina."

"There's no way you would ever be a substitute for Thomas." Myles visibly recoiled as if she'd struck him. "We slept in separate bedrooms."

At first Myles thought Zabrina was comparing him to Thomas in bed, and now her revelation that she and her late husband did not share a bed was too much for him to grasp.

He pressed his mouth to her hair. "I really don't want to know what went on between you and Cooper, because what goes on between a man and his wife is sacrosanct. I'm not going to lie and say I don't have feelings for you because I do. I realized that the day I saw you in the restaurant with my sister, and the most difficult decision I've ever had to face in my life was not making love to you Saturday night. You were in my bed, naked and I still couldn't bring myself to touch you. I also have a confession to make."

"What's that?" Zabrina asked.

"I would've asked you to sleep with me even if you hadn't asked first. It doesn't have to be tonight or tomorrow night, but when it happens it will be the right time and we'll both know it."

Zabrina wound her arms around Myles's waist inside his jacket. Hot tears pricked the backs of her eyelids as she struggled to bring her fragile emotions under control. He'd just validated why she'd fallen in love with him so many years before. He'd never put any pressure on her to sleep with him, and when she had finally offered him her innocent body, the shared experience was one she would remember forever.

"Myles?"

"What, baby?"

"Why didn't you marry?" she asked softly.

"If I had found a woman like you, then I'm certain I would've married her."

Zabrina wanted to believe he'd waited for her, that he couldn't forget her just like she couldn't forget him, but she wasn't that vain. What she did believe was that there were people who were destined to be together. It'd been that way with her and Myles.

The song ended, and Myles escorted Zabrina back to their table where Hugh and Rachel were talking quietly to each other. There was something in the way the restaurateur was staring at the attractive blonde that made Myles pause. Hugh had married his high-school sweetheart, but the union had lasted less than three years. He'd admitted to several long-term relationships, but wasn't ready to commit to marrying again.

Hugh came to his feet with Zabrina's approach. "I'm off tonight, but I was just telling Rachel that if you want something that's not on the menu, then I'll prepare it for you."

Rachel shook her head as she ran her fingers through her hair as if fluffing up her curls. Zabrina caught her meaning immediately. "That's not necessary. I'm more than willing to order from the menu."

"I'll order from the menu," Myles said, agreeing with her.

The sommelier arrived with a bottled of chilled champagne and four flutes. Hugh sampled the wine, smiling. "It's very good." The wine steward filled the flutes, nodded, then walked away.

Hugh raised his flute, and the other three followed suit. "Here's to friendship—old and new."

"Old and new," chorused Myles, Rachel and Zabrina, who only took a sip of the champagne. Myles didn't have to concern himself with her overindulging tonight because she didn't like champagne.

Over the next two hours they were served a four-course

dinner that was nothing short of a culinary feast. The lobster bisque, the mixed green salad with the restaurant's secret vinaigrette, the parmesan-roasted asparagus, prime rib, stuffed pork chops, almond-crusted salmon and the dessert of vanilla gelato topped with puréed cherries, grated lemon zest and ground cinnamon left everyone pushing away from the table.

Hugh, who admitted he didn't dance, sat talking quietly to Rachel while Zabrina and Myles joined other couples gliding across the dance floor. It was close to eleven when Zabrina said she was ready to leave. Her calves were aching from dancing nonstop in four-inch heels.

They said their goodbyes to Hugh, who insisted they not remain strangers. He kissed Zabrina's hand, then Rachel's. "You don't have to wait for Myles to bring you back. Both of you are welcome at any time."

Rachel gave him a demure smile. "It may be a while because I heard there's a three-week wait for a reservation."

Reaching into his jacket, Hugh took out a business card, jotted down a number and handed the card to Rachel. "That's the number to my cell. Call and let me know when you're coming, and I will make certain there will be a table for you."

A rush of color flooded Rachel's face. "Thank you, Hugh."

He leaned over and kissed her cheek. "You're welcome, Rachel."

Hugh walked them to the parking lot, then waited for the valet to bring Myles's SUV around, waving until the taillights disappeared from view.

Myles walked the short distance from Rachel's house to Zabrina's, finding her in the kitchen, barefoot, filling a glass with water from the dispenser on the refrigerator door. Slipping out of his suit jacket, he draped it over the back of a counter stool.

"We have to do it again."

Zabrina jumped and water sloshed out of the glass and onto the floor. She hadn't heard Myles come into the kitchen. She blew out a breath. "What are you trying to do? Give me a heart attack?"

"No. Next time I'll make some noise. Let me do that," he said when she reached for a paper towel to blot up the water. Easing the wad of paper from her fingers, Myles wiped the splatter. A mysterious smile parted his lips when Zabrina stared up at him. "After you drink your water I want you to go upstairs and pack a bag with a change of clothes and whatever else you'll need for a couple of days."

Her eyebrows flickered. "Where am I going?"

He took a step. "You're coming home with me."

"To do what, Myles?" Zabrina's husky voice had dropped an octave.

"I'll let you decide that."

"What if all I want to do is eat and sleep?"

"Then that's what we'll do."

Zabrina took a step, pressing her chest to his. "So, the choice is mine?"

"The choice has always been yours, Brina. If the choice had been mine we would've looked forward to celebrating our eleventh wedding anniversary and Adam would've been an Eaton, not a Cooper."

She decided not to respond to his baiting. "What about your nieces?"

"What about them, Brina?"

"Aren't they coming over to see their puppies?"

Lowering his head, Myles nuzzled the side of her neck.

"My mother took them to Martha's Vineyard to spend some time with Griffin's parents. They're not expected back until Sunday. And that gives us at least three full days and nights to hang out together."

"That sounds like a plan."

"I thought you'd like it. When do you expect Adam to come home?"

Glancing up over her shoulder, Zabrina smiled at the man pressed against her back. Unconsciously, as if they'd rehearsed and choreographed a dance, they'd reverted to their familiar embrace of her settling easily against his body. It felt so good to have him touch her without the artifice of dancing together. She knew they couldn't relive the past, but she planned to enjoy whatever time was given to them. Even if it was only one night, then she would have the memory of that night to hold on to forever.

Just like life, there were no guarantees, no promises of tomorrow. If she and Myles were to have a second chance she would count it as an added blessing. If not, then she would continue to improve on the new life she'd made for herself and her son.

"He's not expected back until the end of July. But I told my aunt to call me and I'll drive down and pick him up if he starts complaining that he wants to come home."

Myles wrapped his arms around her waist. "Do you miss him?"

"I miss him a lot more than I'm willing to admit. I realize he's getting older and he can't remain a mama's boy for the rest of his life, so that's why I agreed to let him spend a month in Virginia."

She missed Adam and she'd missed Myles. Resting her head on his shoulder, Zabrina closed her eyes. Time stood

still as she reveled in the moment where words were un-
necessary. Although she didn't want to move she realized
she wouldn't be able to avoid the inevitable. It was she
who'd issued the challenge when she'd asked Myles to
make love to her. Little had she known that he was contemplating the same if she hadn't been so impulsive.
Whoever made the first move no longer mattered, because
she and Myles wanted the same thing.

They were adults—very consenting adults who weren't
looking for that elusive happy-ever-after ending. They
would engage in a summer tryst and when it ended it would
be without angst or expectations of something. Zabrina
wasn't looking for more. She just wanted to relive a small
part of her past when her cloistered world had been perfect
for a young woman with stars in her eyes.

"Are you going to sleep on me, baby?"

She smiled. "No. You're a drug, Myles Eaton." *A very
potent, habit-forming drug,* she mused.

He chuckled softly, the deep, warm sound caressing
Zabrina's ear. "Will you please explain that very peculiar
assessment of yours truly."

"With you I'm always relaxed. I can always be myself."

"Are you saying you couldn't be yourself as Mrs.
Thomas Cooper?"

"What I'm saying is that I wasn't permitted to be me.
After Thomas's accident I thought of reverting to my maiden
name, but I didn't want it to cause a problem for Adam."

"Why would that pose a problem for him, Brina?"

"He told me that he was glad that he had the same last
name as his mother. So many mothers of his classmates
have different surnames because they've been married two
and sometimes three times. Some of the kids were very

confused about the whole multiple-marriage and blended-family dynamics."

"That's a heavy topic for a young boy to concern himself with."

"When you meet my son you'll know why he thinks the way he does."

Myles wanted to tell Zabrina that he didn't want to meet her son, because it would reopen an emotional wound that had taken a long time to heal. "I'm looking forward to meeting him." It wasn't a complete lie. He wanted to meet the boy who was the light of Zabrina's life. "But, right now I'm contemplating doing unspeakable acts with his gorgeous, sexy mother. You'd better go upstairs and pack or we'll end up on the kitchen floor or countertop, and that will prove disastrous because I don't have any protection on me."

Zabrina wanted to tell Myles that it wouldn't be a bad thing. He'd gotten her pregnant once, and if she were to have another child, then she wanted it to be his. Perhaps this time it would be a girl, then Adam could have the sister he'd been asking for.

When he asked her for a sibling, it was always a sister, which stunned Zabrina because she'd thought he'd want a younger brother. But Adam wisely said he didn't want to have to share his computer games with his brother, while his sister would rather play with her dolls and other girly things.

Easing out of Myles's embrace, she stood on her tiptoes and brushed her mouth against his. "Don't run away."

"I can't…" Myles swallowed the other words poised on the tip of his tongue. He wanted to tell Zabrina he couldn't walk away from her even if his life was in jeopardy, that he planned to spend as much time with her as his or her schedule permitted until the end of summer.

Zabrina waited for him to finish his sentence, but when he didn't she walked out of the kitchen, leaving him staring at her back.

Myles knew he had to be careful, very, very careful or he would find himself so deeply involved with his former fiancée that he wouldn't be able to easily distance himself when it came time to return to Pittsburgh. What he had to continually remind himself of was her deception, and despite not being able to forget Zabrina he knew for certain that he would never forgive her.

Chapter 9

Myles sat on the porch, waiting for Zabrina. Streetlamps that harkened back to nineteenth-century gaslights glowed eerily along the streets that made up the subdivision. A slight smile lifted the corners of his mouth. Someone had left bicycles and skateboards on the lawn of a house across the street without fear they wouldn't find them the next day.

Zabrina had chosen the perfect community in which to raise a child, unlike some neighborhoods where the sound of gunfire and the sight of crime-scene tape were all too familiar. He and his siblings were more than lucky to have had Dwight and Roberta Eaton as their parents—they were blessed.

Roberta, who had given up her career as a teacher to stay at home with her children, said she'd never regretted the decision because she'd utilized her skills when she taught them to read before they were enrolled in kindergarten. There was no trying to circumvent completing homework or a school project because Bertie Eaton was always there to offer her assistance.

And the worst thing about having a doctor and a teacher for parents was that he couldn't feign not feeling well to get out of going to school. A quick examination from Dr. Dwight Eaton verified whether he was well enough to attend classes, and if not, then Bertie would make arrangements to pick up homework assignments. He'd grown up with the constant reminder that he was an Eaton, and he must not do anything to disgrace the family name.

His great-grandfather came to Philadelphia as a young boy during the Great Migration from the South. Daniel Eaton worked two jobs all his life to give his children what had eluded him—a college education. Myles's grandfather earned a law degree from Howard University and three of his five sons followed in his footsteps when they became lawyers, while the other two earned medical degrees. The five brothers married women who were teachers, establishing the criteria for future generations to select a career in medicine, law or education.

He found it ironic that he'd come back to Philadelphia to spend the summer with his family for the first time in over a decade, but they'd all left town: Chandra had flown out of Philadelphia International earlier that morning for a return flight to Belize, his parents had taken their granddaughters to Cape Cod to join their paternal grandparents, and Belinda and her husband were in the Caribbean for a two-week honeymoon. He'd teased his mother, saying he hoped his presence hadn't scared everyone away. Roberta Eaton's response was that she never planned anything for the summer because Dwight would always surprise her with impromptu mini vacations.

The soft click of the door closing garnered Myles's attention. Rising to his feet, he saw that Zabrina had cleansed her face of makeup and brushed her hair off her face. Tank top, cropped pants and a pair of mules had replaced her slacks, blouse and heels.

Zabrina handed Myles a large weekender travel bag. "I'm sorry I took so long. I had to shower and shampoo the gel from my hair."

He dropped a kiss on her damp hair. "That's all right, baby. I was just sitting here taking in the sights."

She inhaled the fragrance of blooming white flowers that opened at nightfall. The sound of an owl's hooting joined the cacophony of crickets serenading the countryside. "I love sitting out at night. One time I fell asleep on the chaise and probably wouldn't have gotten up if a bug hadn't crawled into my nose. Talk about snorting and slinging snot."

Throwing back his head, Myles laughed at the top of his lungs. "That's something I would've paid to see."

She swatted at him. "That's not right, Myles Eaton."

"It serves you right. Remember the time I begged you to go camping with me and you said you were a city girl? Well, that little bug was paying you back for dissing his folks."

Zabrina flashed an attractive moue. "I'm still a city girl."

Putting his arm around her waist, Myles pulled her closer. "Come on, city girl. It's way past my curfew."

"What's the matter, doll face, can't hang?"

"You're going to pay for that remark."

Zabrina wiggled her fingers. "Ooo-oo. I'm so scared."

"You should be." He led Zabrina off the porch to where he'd parked his vehicle. "Speaking of hanging, I'd like to go shopping tomorrow so I can buy you a housewarming gift."

"Thank you, but I don't need anything."

Myles held open the passenger-side door, waiting until Zabrina was seated before he rounded the Range Rover and got in beside her. "Yeah, you do."

"What do I need?"

"A hammock."

Averting her gaze, Zabrina stared out the side window as Myles backed out of the driveway. The Eatons had put up an enormous hammock on their back porch and she'd lost count of the number of times she'd fallen asleep in Myles's embrace after they'd read to each other. For Zabrina it was the novels of Jane Austen, and for Myles it was C. S. Forester. Forester's *The African Queen* was her favorite, along with the 1951 film adaptation starring Katharine Hepburn and Humphrey Bogart.

"A hammock would be nice."

"Don't sound so enthusiastic, Brina."

"I don't mean to sound ungrateful."

"Then what's the matter?"

She turned and stared at his distinctive profile. "It's about us, Myles."

"What about us, Zabrina?"

"We can't go back and redo the past, or right the wrongs."

The muscles in Myles's forearm hardened beneath the sleeve of his shirt as the fingers of his right hand tightened on the leather-wrapped steering wheel in a death grip. "When did you become so vain? My offer to give you the hammock has nothing to do with my attempt to relive the past. I just thought your son and his friends would enjoy it."

A blush crept into her cheeks, flaming with humiliation when Zabrina realized her faux pas. Had she read more into Myles's offer to give her a hammock because she was hoping he would forgive her and they would pick up where they'd left off before her damning telephone call?

How, she thought, had she been so silly, so out of touch with reality? Did she actually believe he would be able to trust her again after she'd not only humiliated him, but also his family?

She was angry and annoyed, angry with Myles because of his acerbic retort about her attempting to flatter herself. And she was annoyed at herself for being embarrassed. "I'm certain Adam will enjoy the hammock."

Myles gave Zabrina a quick glance before maneuvering into the driveway of his sister's house. He knew by the set of her jaw that she was upset. Well, she wasn't the only one. He didn't want to deceive Zabrina or himself into believing they could pick up where they'd left off. Not one to say never, Myles knew *if* he and Zabrina were to start over the impetus would have to be life-changing.

Zabrina stared out the windshield as Myles cut the engine. She hadn't moved when he got out and came around to assist her. Her body was rigid, stiff enough to break into a thousand tiny slivers if she'd been glass, and she chided herself for agreeing to spend the night with Myles. She stood off to the side when he unlocked the door, deactivated the security alarm, then extended his hand.

Myles saw Zabrina staring at his hand as if it were a venomous reptile. Her expression was one he remembered well. He and Zabrina rarely argued, only because she refused to argue. She said it was futile to debate someone whose profession it was to argue cases. Rather than concede defeat, she remained silent. And the silence was more effective than any spoken word.

"I'm sorry for saying what I said about you being vain, because I of all people should know there isn't a vain bone in your body."

Zabrina rolled her eyes at him. "Say it like you mean it, Myles."

A hint of a smile softened his mouth at the same time as he took a step. Myles angled his head and brushed a kiss over her parted lips. "I'm really sorry, baby. Will you forgive me?"

Zabrina bit back a smile. "I'll think about it."

He kissed her again. "Don't think too long. After all, you did promise to give me the next three days, and I'd hate to have to spend the time with you giving me the silent treatment."

Myles might have changed, but not so much that he could deal with Zabrina shutting him out. Whenever they disagreed on something she would stop talking, claiming his debating skills far exceeded hers. He'd tried to tell her that it wasn't about debating but about talking things out. He hadn't wanted her to agree with him on everything as much as he wanted her to see more than one side of a particular topic. As a trial attorney he was expected to sway a jury to believe his client's innocence, yet his powers of persuasion were lost on his fiancée.

Myles exhaled a breath. It'd been a very long time since he'd thought of Zabrina as his fiancée. Perhaps if he'd allowed himself to become more involved with some of the women he'd dated over the years, then he would've been able to completely get her out of his system.

Zabrina placed her palm on Myles's outstretched hand, smiling when his strong fingers closed over hers. The calluses from his martial arts training still hadn't faded completely. She'd loved seeing him compete as much as he'd disliked competing. Her breath would catch in her throat when he walked into the center of the arena, bow to his opponent, then, in lightning-quick fashion, take him off his feet. The day he received his black belt she celebrated with the Eatons when they all went out to dinner at a restaurant featuring Asian cuisine.

Myles pulled her gently into the circle of his embrace, resting his chin on the top of her head. "How you doo-in?" he asked in his best New York inflection.

Zabrina smiled. "It's all good."

"I have to take a shower, so you can either wait up for me or go straight to bed."

She let out an audible sigh. They were about to embark on something she couldn't have predicted the night she'd met Belinda Eaton at the fundraising dinner. Belinda hadn't mentioned Myles and she hadn't asked because she didn't want to hear that he'd married and fathered children, children that should've been theirs.

"I'm going to turn in. My legs feel as if someone pounded them with a mallet."

Lifting his head, Myles pulled back and stared into the pools of brown and gold. "I'll give you a full body massage."

"How much are you going to charge me?" Zabrina teased.

"I'll try and think of something comparable to what a masseur would charge for house calls."

"Can you give me a hint, because I may not have enough money with me?"

Myles's expression went from soft and open to sober within seconds. "I don't want or need your money. And if you ever forget that I'll make certain to remind you."

Zabrina was successful in not visibly flinching as his

words hit her like stones hurled from a sling shot. Her eyes turned cold and frosty again. "What do you want from me other than the sex I'm willingly offering?"

"What about the truth, Zabrina?"

She was taken aback by his demand. "I've told you all I can tell you at this time."

Zabrina knew she hadn't been completely honest with Myles not because she didn't want to be but because she couldn't. The first time she'd lied to Myles it was to protect her father, and she continued to lie to protect her son. How much more pain would he have to experience before reaching adulthood? As a parent it was her responsibility to protect her child, and she would do so until Adam was an adult, even if it meant forfeiting her life.

Myles knew Zabrina was hiding something and he was certain it had something to do with Thomas Cooper. He wanted answers but not at the risk of alienating her. What he had was time—almost eight weeks—in which to wait and watch for her to let down her guard. "If that's the case, then I have to respect your decision."

"Thank you, Myles." Zabrina was relieved he'd decided not to push the issue.

"Why don't you go in and I'll bring in your bag."

Zabrina walked into her childhood friend's living room. The pale carpeting and fabric were a testament that Belinda hadn't decorated her home with children in mind. Walls painted a soothing powder blue were the perfect contrast to the off-white sofa and chairs. The color was repeated in the silk throw pillows and the trim on the off-white rug. Milk-glass vases in varying heights lined the fireplace mantel. White trim on the mantel and French doors emphasized the room's architectural details.

She and Belinda used to spend hours fantasizing about the homes they wanted when they married, and Zabrina never would've imagined that she would become mistress of Cooper Hall. She would've traded everything—the mansion, fancy clothes, priceless pieces of jewelry and the allowance Thomas deposited into an account for her to keep the household running smoothly—to live in a hovel with Myles Eaton.

"Brina?"

She turned to find Myles standing at the entrance to the living room, cradling her quilted bag to his chest. "Yes."

"Come. I'll show you to the bedroom."

Her heart beating a staccato tattoo against her ribs, Zabrina closed the distance between her and Myles. She hadn't felt this anxious even when she'd decided to sleep with Myles for the first time.

"Let's do this," she whispered.

"Whoa. Wait a minute, Brina. Do you hear yourself?"

"What are you talking about?"

"Why are you making it sound as if this is a paid assignation? As if you're offering yourself up to me for a price?"

"Myles, don't. You have no idea what it took for me to ask you to go to bed with me."

Myles's expression was one of restraint and patience. "Stop beating up on yourself, Zabrina. Didn't I tell you that I would've asked you if you hadn't asked me? And if you hadn't had too much to drink Saturday night there is no doubt you would not have left the hotel room without my making love to you. When I saw you with that…that dude I wanted to beat the crap out of him."

With wide eyes, Zabrina searched Myles's face for a hint of guile. "Why? He didn't do anything to you, or to me."

"I was jealous, Brina. I was jealous as hell because he was touching you."

She shook her head in an attempt to bring her fragile emotions under control. She loved Myles, always had and always would, but if Myles was jealous of her and Bailey Mercer then his feelings for her went deeper than he'd admitted.

"You don't ever have to be jealous of me with another man."

Reaching out, Myles cradled her chin in his hand, raising her face to where it was inches from his. "What about Cooper, Brina? Shouldn't I have been jealous of him, too?"

Zabrina pulled her lip between her teeth, increasing the pressure until she felt it pulsing in pain. "No. Remember, I told you we had separate bedrooms."

Raven orbs narrowed under a sweep of inky-black eyebrows. "You never slept with him?"

"Yes, we did sleep together *very* early in the marriage," she answered truthfully. She and Thomas had shared a bed the night they were married. They'd occupied a luxury suite following the private ceremony and the reception dinner at the Sheraton Society Hill Hotel. The beauty and understated elegance of the hotel set on a cobblestone street in Society Hill had failed to offset her dark mood. They'd checked out the following morning and Zabrina had moved into her suite of rooms at Cooper Hall where she didn't have to share a bed with her husband.

It wasn't what Zabrina said, but what she didn't say that tugged at Myles's heart. Not only did she crave physical fulfillment but her loneliness was a result of lack of companionship. Senator Thomas Cooper had earned the rep-

utation of looking out for the residents of the Commonwealth of Pennsylvania—everyone but his wife and son.

He smiled and the gesture was as intimate as a kiss.
"Let's go to bed, darling."

Zabrina followed Myles to the rear of the house where
walls of French doors covered with silk panels opened up
to a bedroom. He touched a wall switch and the space was
flooded with soft light from table lamps with pale blue
pleated shades. Every piece of furniture and all the acces-
sories were in varying shades of white. The absence of
color in the bedroom was offset by the calming blues in
the adjoining sitting/dressing room with blue-and-white-
striped cushions on a white chaise. A blue-and-white-
checked tablecloth on a small table with two pull-up chairs
created the perfect spot for breakfast or afternoon tea.

"It's so beautiful." She couldn't disguise the excitement
in her voice.

Myles set her bag on the carpeted floor next to a bedside
table. "Belinda moved her bedroom downstairs when she
gave Layla and Sabrina the run of upstairs. There are two
half baths in each of what used to be their bedrooms and
a full bath on the second floor. There's also a half bath off
the kitchen with a shower stall that I've commandeered, so
you can have any of the ones upstairs."

Zabrina's gaze widened when Myles slipped out of his
tie and suit jacket, and she prayed he wouldn't undress in
front of her. Although she was more than familiar with his
body, she still didn't feel completely comfortable with
him. Too much time had elapsed for her to pick up where
they'd left off before.

"I'll try and wait up for you."

Myles winked at her. "Remember, I owe you a full-body massage."

She returned the wink. "If that's the case, then I'll make certain to stay awake."

Tossing his jacket and tie on the chair in the sitting area, he turned and walked out of the bedroom. Zabrina sprang into action when she opened her weekender, removing the nightgown she'd packed on top of the bag. She'd showered, shampooed her hair and brushed her teeth in the hope she would have less physical contact with Myles before sharing a bed.

She undressed, pulled the nightgown over her head and slipped between the sheets. Reaching over, she turned off the lamp on her side of the bed and waited for Myles.

Chapter 10

Zabrina hadn't realized she'd dozed off while waiting for Myles to join her in bed until the heat from his body warmed into hers. Stretching languidly like a cat, she smiled and snuggled against his length.

"What took you so long?"

With his arm around Zabrina's waist, Myles pulled her closer, fitting his groin to the roundness of her hips. "I was only gone about fifteen minutes."

"That was fourteen minutes too long."

He nuzzled her neck, inhaling the lingering scent of her perfume. The fragrance wasn't the same as the one she'd worn years before. It was more sophisticated, more woodsy than floral. Zabrina had matured and so had her perfume.

"You're demanding."

"Weren't you the one who said that if you want something, then demand it."

He smiled. "Yes, I did. How are your legs?"

"Better, now that I'm not standing on them."

"Do you still want that massage?"

"Yes please."

Myles shifted, rising to his knees and eased Zabrina to lie on her belly. "When did you start wearing nightgowns to bed?" The white cotton garment with narrow straps crisscrossing her back was sensual and virginal. And because it concealed the curves of her slender body he found it was more provocative than a sheer garment.

Resting her head on her folded arms, Zabrina sighed softly. "I started when I became pregnant. Walking around naked with a big belly wasn't a nice sight. I couldn't bring myself to look in the mirror until I was fully dressed."

Sliding to the foot of the bed, Myles began massaging her ankles. "That all depends on who's looking at the belly."

"What are you talking about?"

"I find pregnant women very sexy. They're like beautiful ripe fruit bursting with life."

Zabrina moaned softly when his strong fingers kneaded the tight muscles in her calves. "You wouldn't have said that about yours truly."

"I'm certain you were beautiful, Brina."

She moaned again. Myles's hands had moved from her calves to her thighs. "That feels so good."

Myles concentrated on the tight muscles in Zabrina's legs and thighs, his fingers working their healing magic. He remembered another time when he'd given her a full-body massage. It was the day after he'd taken her virginity.

Zabrina had complained that every muscle in her body ached, and after giving her a bath he'd dried her off and gently massaged muscles she'd never had to use and muscles she didn't know she had.

Instead of returning home during spring break, Myles had arranged for Zabrina to meet him in Virginia Beach. They'd checked into a hotel, ordered room service and spent the week making love. He knew even before she'd offered him the most precious gift a woman could give a man that he was inexorably and hopelessly in love with Zabrina Mixon.

Reaching up, he pulled her arms down to her sides to make it easier for him to slide the straps of the nightgown off her shoulders. The skin on her back was flawless. The glow from the lamp on his side of the bed had turned her into a statue of molten gold. Sliding a hand under her belly, Myles eased her off the mattress while effortlessly removing the nightgown. It was the second time in a week that she'd lain in his bed while he undressed her. He smiled. It was a habit he could very easily get used to.

Zabrina gasped when she felt the brush of Myles's penis over her buttocks. The hidden place between her legs grew warm, moist. She smothered a moan. It'd been so long, much too long since she'd felt the pleasurable sensations. Her libido had gone into overdrive during her confinement, but after she'd delivered Adam she felt absolutely nothing. Viewing an erotic film or reading erotic literature did nothing to arouse her and she was resigned to believing that she would never feel desire again. But Myles had proven her wrong. She felt desire, and being with him made her feel feminine, sexy.

"Am I hurting you?" Myles asked in her ear. He'd straddled her body while supporting his greater weight on his arms.

Zabrina moaned again, this time as a rush of moisture bathed her core. "No."

She bit her lip to keep from begging him to end the sensual torment that made her feel as if she were coming out of her skin.

Myles didn't know how long he could continue to touch Zabrina without being inside her, because it was becoming more difficult with each passing minute to keep from spilling his passion on the sheets. He'd become aroused the instant he'd walked into the bedroom to find her in his bed. It'd been a long time since he'd experienced an instantaneous erection. It hadn't happened since he was an adolescent.

Then he'd lost count of the number of times he'd embarrassed himself whenever he saw a girl he liked. Rather than approach or say anything to her he'd walk away before she noticed the bulge in his pants.

By the time he'd begun sleeping with Zabrina he was totally in control of his body. Even when other women brushed up against him or leaned over to permit him an eyeful of breasts, he did not react. He realized then that it was the brain that dictated sexual desire. No matter how provocatively a woman dressed or flirted, if he wasn't attracted to her then she couldn't arouse him.

He pressed a kiss on Zabrina's shoulder. "You've lost weight."

"Not that much," she mumbled.

Myles's thumbs moved over her spine. "You're thinner now than when we were together."

"I haven't lost my booty."

"It's still not as full as it used to be."

Zabrina raised her head, peering at Myles over her shoulder. "I thought you were a leg man."

He smiled, flashing straight white teeth. "I like legs, but I like tits and ass, too."

"Myles!"

"What's the matter, baby?"

"I have never known you to refer to a woman's breasts as tits."

His hands stilled, his eyebrows lifting. "I may never have said it around you, but if you're offended then I'll say *T* and *A*."

Her cheeks flamed. "I'm not a prude, Myles."

"Out of bed, yes. In bed, no."

The heat in her face increased. Zabrina never saw herself as prudish. She'd thought of herself as reserved. Perhaps her aloof persona came from being raised by her father and not her mother. Isaac Mixon presented himself as a gentleman in every sense of the word. He was elegant, erudite and had impeccable manners.

Being Isaac's daughter had its advantages and disadvantages. His political savvy permitted him entrée into social circles that someone with lesser clout would never have broached. She was introduced to the sons and nephews of the political elite and if she hadn't been so besotted with Myles there was no doubt she would've accepted the advances of some of the young men destined for careers in public service.

What she'd come to detest was performing as hostess for her father. Men, most old enough to be her father and grandfather whispered licentious comments to her in the hope she would take them up on their ribald suggestions. One man in particular pursued her relentlessly until she deliberately poured a drink in his lap. He called her a bitch, and unfortunately for him Isaac overheard the slur. Two other men had to restrain her father, while the lecherous cretin made his escape.

Myles lowered himself until he lay prone over Zabrina's slight frame. "You feel and smell so good, baby."

Zabrina welcomed his weight. "I've missed you so much."

There was so much emotion in her declaration that Myles felt his heart miss a beat before resuming. She missed him and he'd missed her. He closed his eyes. "I've missed you, too."

"Will you make love to me, Myles Eaton?"

A beat passed. "Yes, I will." Rising slightly, Myles turned Zabrina onto her back. A slight frown appeared between his eyes when he saw hers filling with tears. "No, baby. Please don't cry."

Tears were his Achilles' heel. If Zabrina had come to him instead of calling him with the news that she was ending their engagement, Myles knew he wouldn't have taken it so hard. Even if he hadn't been able to get her to change her mind at least he would've been given the opportunity to challenge her. And if she'd cried he would've forgiven her and wished her the best.

The call was impersonal, and her voice that of a stranger. There was little or no emotion in her voice when she recited what sounded like a rehearsed script. Stunned, he'd hung up, shutting out her monotone and closing the book on the sensual adventure he'd shared with the woman he'd wanted to spend the rest of his life with. And despite her sweet deception, Zabrina was back, back in his life and back in his bed.

Zabrina closed her eyes, hoping to stem the tears pricking the backs of her eyelids. "I'm not crying because I'm sad, Myles."

He pressed his mouth over one eye, then the other, tasting salt. "Then why are you crying?"

"I'm happy, darling. The last time I felt this way was when I saw my son for the first time."

Myles went still. "Did he abuse you?"

Zabrina opened her eyes. "What are you talking about?"

"Did Cooper abuse you?"

She dropped her gaze, staring at his bare chest. "Physically, no."

"So, he abused you emotionally." The question was a statement.

Zabrina shook her head. "I can't explain it, Myles. Our marriage was very strange, and that's all I'm going to say about it. Thomas is gone and I'm free, free to live my life on my own terms."

Burying his face between her neck and shoulder, Myles breathed a kiss there. He'd gone to bed with women where a third person was in bed with them because they hadn't been able to exorcise former husbands or boyfriends. Their inability to let go had doomed their relationships from the start. Zabrina's declaration that she was free to live her life on her terms meant there were no ghosts from her past to interfere with their summer liaison.

"We can't right the wrongs or turn back the clock," he said in a quiet voice, "but what we can do is heal."

Zabrina had begun to heal the day she'd become a widow. Any power Thomas Cooper had over her died with him. Surprisingly, she'd never wished him dead, but for him to fall from grace.

Smiling, she wrapped her arms around Myles's neck. "Sometimes, counselor, you talk much too much."

He winked at her. "What would you have me do instead?"

Pulling his head down, she pressed her mouth to his. "This. And this." Zabrina kissed him under an ear.

"That's nice."

She bit down on his lower lip, suckling it and simulating his making love to her and achieving the response she sought when Myles moved his hips against hers. "How was that?"

Myles leaned over, opening the drawer to the bedside table and removing a condom. If he didn't put on protection now he knew it wouldn't happen, and what he didn't want was to get Zabrina pregnant. He'd used protection when they'd begun sleeping together. However, once she went on the pill their lovemaking had become more frequent, more spontaneous and more intense.

With the latex sheath in place, he began the journey to reacquaint himself with her body. Every muscle in his body screamed, vibrated. The scent of the perfume on her silken skin rose sharply in his nostrils, heating his blood as Myles fell headlong into the lust holding him captive. He kissed her forehead, her nose, her mouth, then moved lower to her throat where a pulse beat erratically as her breathing quickened.

Zabrina was hot, then cold and then hot again. The pleasure Myles wrung from her was pure and unrestrained. The sexual passion of her body after years of celibacy had been awakened and she wanted him, all of him inside her.

"Please, Myles."

"What, baby?"

"Don't make me wait."

"I thought you liked foreplay."

She was on fire. Feelings she'd thought dead were back, making her aware of the strong passion within her. All memories of being held in Myles's protective embrace, the pure, unrestrained ecstasy that took her beyond herself and the pleasurable aftermath of a shared lovemaking that made them cease to exist as separate entities came to mind. She liked and wanted foreplay, but not now, not after ten long, lonely years during which she'd had to deny being female.

Her fists pounded his back. "Ditch the foreplay, Myles! I need you! Now!"

Myles wanted foreplay, a long, leisurely exploration of the body he'd fantasized about whenever he took another woman to bed. Their faces had become Zabrina's, their bodies Zabrina's, and whenever he climaxed it was her name that resounded in his head. She'd been so indelibly imprinted in his heart that he found himself comparing every woman to her.

It'd gotten so bad that he'd consciously embarked on a quest to see how many women he could bed before exorcising Zabrina Mixon, but he'd scrapped it because he thought of his sisters and of some man taking advantage of them.

He'd lectured Donna, Belinda and Chandra, telling them he would commit capital murder if any man harmed them. It took a while, but he realized it'd been the wrong thing to say to them; whenever they ended a relationship they were reluctant to talk about it.

Grasping his erection, he pushed gently into her vagina, increasing the pressure until a small cry from Zabrina stopped him. She was tight, tighter than he'd remembered. He was only halfway inside her. "Easy, Brina. Try to relax."

"I am," she gasped in sweet agony and unable to believe the tumult of intense pleasure holding her captive, refusing to let her go.

Still joined, Myles cupped her hips, lifting her body off the mattress and in one, sure thrust of his hips her body accepted every inch of him, both of them sighing in unison. He felt her flesh pulsing around his, pulling him in farther.

Zabrina wrapping her legs around his waist had become Myles's undoing. It was his favorite position because it permitted deeper penetration. She'd missed him and he'd missed her. He missed the intimacy, the shared moment when they became one and the lingering pulsing aftermath of the shared ecstasy where no words were needed to communicate with each other.

Zabrina prayed she wasn't dreaming and that when she woke she wouldn't be alone in bed. After her first trimester she'd experienced a resurgence of sexual desire that was frightening. She went to bed crying for Myles to come and lie beside her, and when her crying jag ended the dreams took over. Erotic dreams where she relived making love with him and her body reacted. She woke to intense orgasms, the walls of her vagina contracting and her body drenched in moisture. The dreams continued nightly until she woke one morning to intense pain in her lower back. When the pains continued unabated she knew she was in the early stages of labor.

The dreams stopped altogether after Adam's birth, and as much as she tried, she couldn't conjure up any erotic images to assuage her sexual frustration. After a while, she stopped trying and embraced celibacy as if it were her fate.

Myles wasn't a dream, the strength in the hands gripping her hips was real and the hard, engorged penis moving in and out of her in a measured cadence was beyond real.

Desire rose so quickly that Zabrina felt as if she was caught in a maelstrom of sexual hysteria bordering on insanity. She wanted to move, but Myles, holding her fast, wouldn't permit movement as he quickened his thrusts. The raspy sound of his labored breathing against her ear escalated. He began chanting and it took a full minute before she could understand what he was saying.

"Baby, oh baby, baby, baby," Myles crooned over and over when he felt the buildup of pleasure at the base of his spine. He knew it was going to be over and he wanted it to go on until he was repaid tenfold for the years when he'd wanted to go to sleep and wake up in Zabrina's arms.

He'd lied to himself at Belinda and Griffin's wedding. He'd wanted their wedding to have been his and Zabrina's. And, although he hadn't met Adam, he wanted the boy to have been his and Zabrina's. All of the things Thomas Cooper shared with Zabrina should've been his. It was as if the man had stolen his life.

He released her hips to grasp her legs and settle her ankles over his shoulders. What he saw in Zabrina's golden gaze sent a wave of fear throughout his body. The expression on her face was one he'd seen countless times in the past. She was still in love with him. She loved him as much as he'd loved and continued to love her.

When she confessed that she hated Thomas Cooper as much as she loved you I knew something wasn't quite right. He hadn't believed Belinda when she'd told him what Zabrina told her.

He also hadn't believed Zabrina when she told him that she wanted him for sex. A woman asking him to sleep with her just for sex made him feel cheap. It was no different than a hooker asking him if he wanted her to show him a good time—for a price. And, Zabrina's price was sexual favors because she was sexually frustrated. After all, she did admit that she and her husband slept in separate bedrooms.

She wanted sex for the summer, whereas he wanted more. And the more was starting over. He wanted to move her and her son to Pittsburgh where people wouldn't recognize her as the widow of Pennsylvania's junior senator.

Myles closed his eyes against her intense stare, not seeing the rush of blood suffusing her face and chest, or the hardening of her nipples and pebbling of her breasts' areolas as an orgasm held her in its grip. It released her at the same time another one swept her up, holding her trapped in a pulsing, pleasurable passion before releasing her to another—this one more turbulent. Her body vibrated liquid fire and Zabrina finally surrendered to the passion as tremors seized her until she shook uncontrollably.

"M-y-l-e-sss!" His name, tumbling from quivering lips, came out in syllables.

Myles answered her entreaty when he ejaculated into the condom. The strong pulsing continued until he collapsed heavily on her body. He lay on Zabrina, helpless as a newborn, while he waited for his heart to stop slamming against his ribs.

He was uncertain how long they lay together, their bodies still joined, but Myles was loath to withdraw from her warmth. He wanted to lie between her scented thighs forever. But he did withdraw, leaving the bed to go into the bathroom to discard the condom, lingering long enough to wash away the evidence of their lovemaking. He took a quick peek at the puppies sleeping atop each other in their crate, then returned to the bedroom.

Zabrina had fallen asleep, her features angelic in repose. He loved her, she loved him and they'd agreed to sleep together for the summer. Where, he mused, would that leave them come summer's end? Would she be willing to

give up her new home and friends to follow him across the state? Or would he be forced to sacrifice his teaching position to go back to practicing law?

Slipping into bed beside Zabrina, he pulled the sheet up over their naked bodies and extinguished the light. Turning on his side, he pressed his chest to her back, rested his arm over her hip and joined her in the sleep reserved for sated lovers.

Chapter 11

Zabrina managed to slip out of bed without waking Myles. She used an upstairs bathroom to shower and dress. The puppies were awake, growling and nipping at each other when she went over to the crate in a corner of the laundry room. A baker's shelf held an assortment of doggie food and supplies. She wasn't certain whether the dogs were permitted the run of the house, so she closed the louvered doors before opening the door to the crate. The Yorkies came at her like fluffy bowling balls, jumping up while trying to lick her face.

"Sorry," she said softly, "but I don't kiss doggies." Without warning, the doors opened and the dogs shot past her.

"That's good to know," said a familiar baritone behind her, "because I'd hate to be charged with animal cruelty because two little fur balls are attempting to hit on my woman."

Zabrina took a quick glance at Myles, finding him incredibly delicious in a pair of gray paisley-print silk boxers. "I know you're not talking about hurting the babies."

Bending slightly, Myles cupped her elbow, easing her up to a standing position. "I will if you decide to bring them into the bed with us."

Seeing the skin crinkled around his eyes told her he was kidding. He was the one who'd grown up with a menagerie of animals in and around the Eaton house, while the building she lived in with her father had a no-pets rule. Myles had his dogs, Donna her rabbits, Belinda her cats and Chandra fish, but the youngest Eaton daughter also had to have baby chicks every Easter. The elder Eatons didn't mind the animals but the rule was the cats and dogs had to be neutered or spayed. Once the rabbits began multiplying they were given to a local pet store. When the baby chicks grew up to become hens and roosters they also found new homes at a farm.

"Do they sleep in the bed with your nieces?"

"No. Belinda was emphatic when she reminded the girls that the first time she found the dogs asleep in their beds will be the last time. Why did you let them out?"

"I was going to clean their crate," Zabrina said.

"I'll clean the crate, and after I take a shower I'll start breakfast."

"While you're doing that I'll take Nigel and Cecil for a walk."

Myles smiled at the woman who'd offered the most exquisite pleasure he'd had in years, resisting the urge to pick her up to take her back to the bedroom. He found her enchanting in the body-hugging jeans, fitted T-shirt and sandals. With her freshly scrubbed face and short hair in sensual disarray, she projected an air of innocence. His gaze lingered on her full lips; he didn't know how it was possible but he felt sexual magnetism radiating from her like sound waves.

Zabrina knew what Myles was thinking because it was the same with her. Making love last night had only served to whet her sexual appetite. After all, she had more than a decade to make up in less than eight weeks. Even if they made love every day for two months it wouldn't put a dent into the number of times they would've made love if they'd been married.

"Please hand me their leashes and harnesses. Now that you've opened the door I'm going to have to go and look for them."

Myles stopped her when he reached for her hand. "Watch."

Pursing his lips, he whistled, the piercing sound reverberating throughout the kitchen. Within seconds the two puppies came sliding across the tiled floor, sitting obediently at his feet while he slipped on the harnesses, attached the leads and handed them to Zabrina.

She flashed a dazzling smile. "I'm impressed."

His smile matched hers, slashes appearing in his lean jaw as he inclined his head. "Thank you, darling."

She kissed the stubble on his chin. "You're welcome, darling. How long do you usually walk them?"

"Half an hour to forty-five minutes."

"Please hand me a couple of poop bags and we'll be on our way."

Zabrina pushed the small plastic bags into a pocket of her jeans and her cell phone into another. The puppies were wiggling, making strange noises and pulling on their leads in their impatience to go outdoors. She led them out a side door and into the warm, sun-filled morning.

Nigel and Cecil stopped every few feet to sniff grass, fire hydrants and lampposts. They took off running when a squirrel raced across the road, but she managed to pull them back to walk beside her. She couldn't whistle between her teeth like Myles, but watching *Dog Whisperer* had come in handy. She'd become a pack leader. There were other people walking their dogs. Some of the canines stopped to sniff the Yorkies and others walked by as if they didn't exist.

I've become a true suburban housewife, she thought. She mentally corrected herself. If she'd married Myles, then she would've become the housewife. Going to bed with Myles, making love, walking dogs and sharing breakfast. That was what she would've had *if* her father hadn't had a gambling problem, if he hadn't stolen from Thomas Cooper and if he hadn't gone to loan sharks to pay off his gambling debts.

The *ifs* assaulted her until she felt like screaming at the top of her lungs. Whenever she recalled the scene with Thomas and his muscle pointing a gun at her father's head she chided herself for giving in too easily.

If the man Thomas called Davidson had killed her father there was no way he could've gotten away with it. If they'd shot her in order to eliminate a witness they still wouldn't have gotten away with it.

Zabrina walked as far as her subdivision before retracing her steps. The puppies weren't as frisky as they'd been when they'd begun their walk. The rising humidity signaled another hazy, hot and humid summer day. Without warning, Cecil and Nigel started running and when she looked down the street she saw Myles sitting out on the porch. Scooping up a puppy under each arm, she approached the house. Myles stood up, came off the porch and took the dogs from her. He looked incredibly sexy in a black tank top and khaki-colored walking shorts. His head came down and she raised her face for his kiss.

"How was your walk?" he whispered against her lips.

"Good."

Myles kissed her again. "As soon as you wash up we can sit down to eat."

Zabrina went into the house, Myles following with Nigel and Cecil. She washed up in the half bath off the kitchen, while the puppies went back into their crate.

She sniffed the air. It smelled like apples. "Something smells delicious. What did you make?"

"Come out and see."

She dried her hands, then walked out of the bathroom and into the kitchen. Myles stood behind a chair in the dining nook, waiting to seat her at the table covered with a linen tablecloth with cross-stitch embroidery.

"Do you want me to set the table?"

Myles's hands circled Zabrina's waist, lifting her to sit on the table. Repositioning the chair, he sat down in front of her. "I just set the table, Brina. Now, I'm going to have my appetizer before we sit down to breakfast."

Zabrina stared at the flecks of gray in his cropped black hair. "What on earth are you talking about?"

Unsnapping the waistband of her jeans, Myles lowered the zipper. Placing his hand over her belly and the other under her head, he eased her back onto the table. Half rising, he loomed over the woman who made him do things he didn't want to do; she made him love her when he had every right to hate her.

"I'm going to do to you now what you wouldn't let me do last night."

Zabrina opened her mouth to protest. The words died on her lips when his mouth covered hers, swallowing her breath. "Myles! No-oo! Please don't."

Her pleas fell on deaf ears and her shame increased. Myles had her jeans and panties down around her knees, his face buried between her thighs, all the while holding her wrists in a strong grip. The first time he'd introduced her to a different form of lovemaking she'd refused to look at him for days, so great was her shame. It was the first and last time Myles had attempted to make love to her with his mouth and tongue. Now, she was at his mercy and the sensations washing over had her feeling as if she were losing touch with reality. Zabrina floated in and out, gasping and sobbing as she attempted to sit up, push his head away, but to no avail.

Like a man seated at a banquet table, Myles feasted on the swollen mounds of flesh at the apex of Zabrina's thighs. Not only did she smell delicious, but she tasted delicious. He caught the engorged bud between his teeth, increasing the pressure until Zabrina's hips came off the surface of the table. Her breath came in deep surrendering moans, her head thrashing from side to side. She arched, fell back and then arched again as moisture pooled into his mouth.

Myles was relentless. He didn't love her flesh, he worshipped her. Without warning it happened. The soft pulsing grew stronger, more intense. The measured contractions shook Zabrina, her legs trembling uncontrollably. But he was ready. Pulling her closer, her hips on the edge of the table, he lifted her until there was no space, no light between his mouth and the entrance to her vagina.

She screamed once. Then again. And again. Her final scream made the hair stand up on the back of his neck, yet he wouldn't give her ease. Myles wanted the memory of his mouth on her to become an indelible tattoo that no other man could eradicate.

Eyes closed, chest heaving, Zabrina lay spent, unable to move. The orgasms had come so quickly, were so intense that her heart had stopped for several seconds and for the first time in her life she had experienced *le petit mort*.

She was still in a prone position when Myles returned with a warm cloth to wash between her legs. "I'm going to pay you back for that stunt."

Myles leaned over her, smiling. "What are you going to do, baby girl?"

"You'll find out soon enough," she teased.

He wiggled his fingers. "I'm scared of you." Wrapping his arm around her waist, he eased her up. "I'm going to clean off the table, then we'll eat."

Zabrina wrinkled her nose. "I'll never look at this table the same way again."

Myles helped her off the table. "And I'll never think of appetizers the same way again."

She landed a soft punch on his shoulder. "When did you become a dirty old man?"

"I wasn't one until I accepted the position to become your sex toy."

Crossing her arms under her breasts, Zabrina angled her head. "Perhaps I should've checked your credentials before I hired you."

"My credentials are impeccable, beautiful."

The sweep hand on the clock over the kitchen sink made a full revolution before she said, "Yes, they are, Myles."

He winked at her. "I made cinnamon waffles with caramelized apples for breakfast."

He remembered, Zabrina thought. Myles had remembered her favorite breakfast food. She loved all types of waffles covered with every fruit imaginable. He'd introduced her to fried chicken and waffles with a tangy honey-strawberry topping, which had become her favorite.

A sad smile touched her mouth. They had the summer in which to recapture a modicum of happiness that promised forever. *I can do it,* she mused. *We can do it.*

Myles set up the oversize hammock between two large trees in the rear of Zabrina's house rather than on the front porch. He was surprised at the size of the lot on which her house had been erected. The subdivision had only ten homes, but if they'd been built on smaller lots the number of structures could've been twice that. It was apparent the developer wanted to give the residents the feel of estate living. If it had been a gated community, then it would've provided maximum security.

Stepping back, he surveyed his handiwork. "Do you want to try it out?"

Zabrina smiled at Myles. "Sure." Sitting on the hammock, she grasped it with her left hand and lifted her left leg, then her right leg and hand until she lay on the tightly slung cord.

Myles applauded softly. "Nice technique."

He remembered the first time Zabrina had attempted to get into the hammock—she'd fallen and hit her head on the floor of the porch. The impact of the fall left her motionless. Too frightened to move her, Myles ran to get his father who was seeing a patient in his home office. Dr. Eaton revived her and personally drove her to the hospital for an evaluation. Isaac Mixon arrived in time to hear the neurosurgeon tell him that his daughter had suffered a mild concussion. It would be another six months before Zabrina attempted to get on the hammock, this time with explicit instructions as to the proper technique.

Smiling, Zabrina beckoned to Myles. "Come, get in with me." She scooted over and he climbed in beside her. Snuggling against his chest, she looped her leg over his bare ones. "This thing is large enough for Adam *and* Rachel's two children."

"You're going to have to show them how to get in and out without falling and breaking something."

She winced. "I can't imagine either of them spending the summer with their arms or legs in a cast. Remember the summer you sat around with your arm in a cast?"

Myles grunted. "Please don't remind me." He'd broken several bones in his right wrist during a martial arts competition. The pain was excruciating yet he'd kept fighting. He won the competition, earned his brown belt and spent the summer sitting around the house watching grass grow. If it hadn't been for Zabrina he believed he would've gone completely mad. Her father dropped her off every morning, and after playing with Belinda she would join him in the hammock to read. Most times she'd end up falling asleep and he'd lie there staring at her.

She'd been so young, so innocent and so untouchable. It was the summer Zabrina Mixon had become more to him than his sister's friend. It was the first time he saw her as a young woman and a companion. Her straight body had developed womanly curves, her voice had changed to a low, smoky quality that caught one's attention the moment she opened her mouth. And, with her jet-black hair and jewellike eyes she had morphed into an incredibly beautiful adolescent.

Things had changed when one of his friends made a crude comment about Zabrina's mouth and what she could do to him. Myles had caught the much taller and heavier boy by the throat within seconds and would have nearly crushed his windpipe if the other boys on the football team hadn't pulled him off. It was the first and last time he touched someone outside the realm of competition. It was also the first time he realized his protective instincts went deeper than taking care of his sisters and Belinda's friend.

Torn by ambivalent feelings, Myles decided going away to college rather than commuting was best because it put some distance between him and a teenage girl. What frightened him more than facing charges of statutory rape was what it would do to his family's reputation and what Isaac Mixon's reaction would be to his taking advantage of his daughter. And he knew he'd made the right decision when Zabrina kissed him. There was nothing chaste or innocent in the kiss, and it was another five years before he sampled the sweetness of her sexy mouth again.

"Brina, baby. Are you falling asleep?"

She stirred. "I was before you called my name."

"Why don't we go inside and lie down?"

"I don't feel like moving."

"It's getting too hot out here." Midday temperatures were already in the high eighties and meteorologists were predicting the mercury was going as high as the mid-nineties.

Rolling over, Zabrina opened an eye and peered at the face close to hers. She always marveled at the length of Myles's eyelashes. Whenever he closed his eyes the tips of his lashes grazed his high cheekbones.

"What do you have planned for the rest of the day?" she asked.

"I'll leave that up to you," Myles countered.

"I've been craving crab cakes."

Myles lifted his expressive eyebrows. "Are you sure you're not pregnant?" he teased.

"Of course I'm sure. You're the only man I've slept with, and I'm expecting my period in a few days, so bite your tongue, Myles Eaton."

"Do you want more children?"

His question startled her. What did he expect her to say? If they'd been married there was no doubt she would've had at least another child, or maybe two more. "Yes."

A silence followed her answer as Myles wrestled with his conscience. He'd always wanted children, and he'd wanted Zabrina to be the mother of his children. "How does Adam feel about you having more children?"

"All he used to talk about was having a sister because the kids in his classes would come to school with the news that they had a new baby brother or baby sister. Now I think he's resigned to being an only child."

"You never liked being an only child."

Zabrina sighed audibly. "I hated it. Belinda was the closest thing to having a sister. After we moved to the city, I used to nag my father so much about spending time with Belinda that he finally gave in and let me come to your house or let her come to mine every weekend."

"Are you thinking of remarrying?"

"No."

"Then how are you going to give your son a brother or sister?"

"Either I'll have an affair and get pregnant, or adopt."

An angry frown settled into Myles's features. "Having an affair is wrong, Brina."

"Why is it wrong, Myles?"

"You would sleep with a man, get pregnant and not let him know you were having his baby?"

With wide eyes, she met his angry glare. *Why not,* she wanted to tell him. *I did it with you.* "That would be best if I didn't want to be bothered with him."

Myles's frown deepened. "What do you mean by not wanting to be bothered with him? Why deal with him in the first place if you don't want to be bothered?"

"Haven't you slept with women you didn't particularly like?"

"No. Every woman I've slept with I liked in one way or another."

"Well, I know men who don't care if they like a woman or not. It's just another warm body for them when they need someone to scratch their itch."

"You'd pick up a complete stranger, lie down with him just to get pregnant?"

"I didn't say that, Myles, so don't try and put words in my mouth."

Myles couldn't believe what he was hearing. This was a side of Zabrina he'd never seen. He couldn't imagine her dating a man, sleeping with him, then walking away when she found herself pregnant.

She was nothing like the young woman who'd parried the advances of other men to *save* herself for him. She'd been very popular in high school. What he'd found startling was that she was liked by boys and girls equally. There were occasions at high school when the more popular the girl was among the boys, the more the other girls lined up against her. Zabrina always had a smile for everyone, diffusing whatever problems she would've faced.

"I'm willing to become a sperm donor if you want another child." The instant the words were out Myles knew he couldn't retract them.

Zabrina stared at the man lying beside her as if he'd taken leave of his senses. "You're crazy!"

"No, Brina, you're the crazy one. Wouldn't it be better to know something about your child's father? I'm disease-free and to my knowledge there have been no crazies in the family tree for the past three generations."

Her eyes grew wider. "Yes, there is. *You're* crazy."

He smiled. "No, I'm not. Here I'm willing to help you out and you tell me I'm crazy. If anyone is crazy, then it's you if you're considering picking up some asshole you know nothing about."

Her temper flared. "The difference between you and some *asshole* is he won't insinuate himself into my life and my children's. And I know you well enough to know you would want to be involved in the lives of your children."

"You know me well, Zabrina," Myles drawled arrogantly. "There's no way I'd walk away from my child or children no matter what the situation between me and their mother."

"That's why you can't become a donor." She held up her hand when Myles opened his mouth to come back at her. "I know we've always gotten along, but I've changed. Things I wanted ten years ago I don't want now."

"Does that include marriage?"

"Yes, it does. Once was enough, thank you very much. And if I do agree to let you father my child there are risks."

"What risks?" he asked.

"That you would sue for custody."

"I'd like joint custody, but I'd never take a child away from his or her mother."

"You say that now, Myles. But, what if I do or say something to piss you off?"

"It still wouldn't happen."

"I can't take that risk," Zabrina said. "After all, you're an attorney and you still have a lot of friends and colleagues who are judges. The odds of me keeping my child are slim to none."

"When did you become so distrustful?" Myles asked with no expression on his face. "There was a time when you trusted me with your life."

She dropped her gaze. "I told you, I've changed."

Rather than agree with her Myles decided to drop the subject. He'd temporarily taken leave of his senses when he'd offered to get Zabrina pregnant. It was *he* who wanted to turn back the clock. What he'd forgotten was there were no do-overs when it came to life. One learned from one's mistakes, and hopefully would not repeat them.

It was apparent he was a slow learner.

Chapter 12

Leaning over the small round table, Zabrina peered at Myles through her lashes. The flickering light from a votive threw long and short shadows over his attractive male features. His large, deep-set dark eyes glowed like polished onyx.

"You didn't have to drive to Baltimore to eat crab cakes, darling."

A hint of a smile touched the corners of his mouth. "If you want authentic Maryland crab cakes, then you go to Maryland. It's just like Philly cheesesteaks or New York pizza. Why settle for an imitation when you can get the real deal."

"So, if I want deep-dish Chicago-style pizza you'll drive there for me?"

Myles angled his head, admiring the woman sitting across the table. When he'd told her they were going out for dinner she'd changed into a flattering rose-pink sleeveless dress that nipped her waist and flared around her knees. The hot summer sun had darkened her face to a rich chestnut brown that brought out a spray of freckles over her nose and cheeks. His gaze lingered on loose tendrils of hair falling over her forehead, then to the rose-pink gloss on her generously curved lips.

Once he thought about his offer to father a child for Zabrina he realized it wasn't as much for her as it was for Myles Adam Eaton. He would celebrate his thirty-ninth birthday in October and turn forty the following year. There was a time when he would've thought his life would be complete at forty and that he would be living the American dream with a wife, children, house and career. He hadn't thought that at his age he would've attained only two of the four.

"Yes, Brina. Have you forgotten that at one time I would've done anything for you?"

She speared a portion of crab, avocado and grapefruit salad with chive vinaigrette but didn't bring the fork to her mouth because she was afraid she would choke on the food. Zabrina closed her eyes, counted to three and then opened them. "No, Myles. I haven't forgotten."

"If that's the case, then why did you ask me?"

She set down her fork, her gaze never leaving Myles's face. It was their first full day together and she felt as if time had stood still, that they'd spent every day of the past ten years together. "I don't know," Zabrina said truthfully. "I keep forgetting that I'm the one that has changed. I'm now Zabrina Cooper and you're still Myles Eaton."

Myles wanted to tell her that she hadn't changed that much, that she'd talked herself into believing that she was different. She may have been more wary, less trustful but their incredible chemistry hadn't changed.

"What's in a name, Brina? Names are changed every day for one reason or another."

Zabrina picked up her fork again and took a bite, savoring the sharpness of torn frisée and radicchio leaves and the semisweet tart taste of sections of pink grapefruit on her tongue.

"You're right," she agreed after swallowing a mouthful of salad.

His expression brightened. "So, finally we agree on something."

"We agree on a lot of things, Myles."

"Enumerate."

"We like each other."

Myles's expression changed, becoming stoic. "I think it's more than liking, Brina."

"What is it?"

"You tell me."

"It can't be love, Myles."

"And why not? There was a time when we were very much in love with each other."

Zabrina saw Myles looking at her as if he were photographing her with his eyes, and wondered if he could see what she'd tried vainly to hide. What she'd tired of was lying to him and to herself. She loved Myles, had always loved and would always love him.

"You're right," she repeated for the second time in a matter of minutes. "We did love each other, and not much has changed." A swollen silence followed her pronouncement. "I'm still in love with you."

Leaning forward, Myles rested an arm on the table.

"You are still in love with me, or you never stopped loving me?"

A sense of strength came to Zabrina as she met his penetrating stare. She'd confessed to Belinda that she loved her brother, and what she hadn't been able to tell him verbally she was able to do with her body. For more than ten long suffering years she'd yearned for Myles, cried herself to sleep, and if it hadn't been for Adam she wasn't certain that she'd have had the will to survive.

"I never stopped loving you, Myles. Is that what you want to hear?"

"No," he replied softly, "it's not so much what I want to hear but what I need to know."

"Why?"

"I just need to know if we're on the same page."

"You don't hate me for what I did to you?" There was no mistaking the astonishment in her voice.

"I didn't hate you, but I did hate how you did it, Brina. If you'd come to me and told me you were interested in someone else I would've given you an out without the embarrassment you caused my family. What was so crazy was that I couldn't even give them an explanation as to why."

"You…you didn't tell them I was in love with someone else?"

All of the warmth in Myles's eyes disappeared, replaced with a cold loathing. "No. I didn't tell them because I didn't believe you. But, then when word leaked out that you'd married Thomas Cooper they had the answer."

"I'm sorry, Myles. I'm so sorry for what I did to you and what your family had to go through because of my deception." Unshed tears shimmered in her eyes.

Myles shook his head. He was confused. Zabrina

admitted that she still loved him, yet she'd told Belinda that she hated Thomas Cooper. Which was it? Had she been in love with him *and* Cooper? Or had she loved Cooper more than she loved him? And he wondered what had happened between her and her husband to force them to occupy separate bedrooms.

"Were you ever in love with Cooper?" he asked. Myles chided himself for asking, but he had to know.

A sad smile trembled over Zabrina's lips. "No, Myles. I was never in love with Thomas Cooper."

He had his answer, but ironically it didn't make him feel any better. "Thank you for your honesty. I suppose you want to know…" Myles's words trailed off when his cell phone rang. Reaching into the breast pocket of his jacket, he stared at the display, then at Zabrina. The call was from a former law-school friend who'd set up an office in North Philly where most of his clients were indigent. Some were illegal immigrants seeking citizenship.

"Answer it, Myles," she urged softly.

"Thanks." He punched a button. "What's up, Willie?" Myles caught and held Zabrina's gaze as he listened to the drawling voice coming through the earpiece. "Look up Miller v. Albright, 1998. The facts are similar to your case. If the couple isn't married, and when the citizen parent is the mother, then the kid is a citizen if the mother meets minimum residency requirements. If the mom is a citizen, and in order for a foreign-born child to be a citizen, then she must have established residence here for a minimum period of time."

"What about the father, Eaton?"

"If the father is a citizen he must prove paternity by clear and convincing evidence, and show evidence of actual relationship with the kid during the period of the child's minority."

"Thanks, man, you just answered my question."

Myles smiled. "I'm glad I could help out."

"How much are you going to charge me, Eaton?"

"Now you know I offer friends the professional courtesy rate," he teased. "Send me seven thousand and we'll be even."

"Sheee-it," Willie drawled. "Even if you were for real, man, I wouldn't be able to pay you. It takes me about six months to pull down seven thousand in fees from clients who walk in off the street."

"How are you keeping the doors open?"

"I have a few private clients on the side."

"How *private*, Willie?"

"Now, Eaton, you should know I can't reveal names. Attorney-client privilege."

Slumping against the back of his chair, Myles stared out the window of the restaurant overlooking Baltimore Harbor. "Don't call me, Willie, when they come for you."

"What are you trying to say, Eaton?"

"You know what I'm trying to say, Willie. Because if your so-called private clients go down you're going with them. I'm glad I was able to help you, but I'm going to end this call because you interrupted my dinner." He tapped a button, ringing off. Exhaling, Myles returned the phone to his jacket. "I'm sorry you had to hear that," he apologized to Zabrina.

"That's okay," Zabrina replied.

He wanted to tell her that it wasn't okay. The call had interrupted what he'd wanted to say to Zabrina, something he knew would change them and his tenuous relationship with her.

"How do you remember all of those cases?" she asked, breaking into his thoughts.

Myles lifted a shoulder. "I don't know," he admitted.

"I suppose it's like a song you've heard over and over. You find yourself singing along without actually thinking of the words."

Propping an elbow on the table, Zabrina rested her chin on the heel of her hand. "Don't be so modest, darling."

Assuming a similar position, he smiled at the incredibly lovely woman sharing the table with him. "You use that term rather loosely."

Her eyebrows lifted. "What term?"

"Darling."

"Does the word make you uncomfortable?"

Myles shook his head, his expression unreadable. His dark eyes caressed her face before his lids shuttered them from her gaze. "No, Brina. There aren't too many things that make me feel uncomfortable. I just need to know if you're calling me *darling* out of habit or if you actually think of me as your darling."

A frown appeared between Zabrina's eyes. "Why are you cross-examining me, Myles?"

"Just answer the question, Zabrina."

"Why?"

The corner of his mouth twisted in frustration. If Zabrina had a negative personality trait it was stubbornness. He'd lost track of how many times he'd walked away from her in exasperation rather than blurt out something that would've ended their relationship. If he pushed, then she pulled and vice versa. It was only in bed where they came together on equal footing.

"I need to know where we're going with our relationship."

"What relationship, Myles? I thought we agreed to sleep together for the summer, and when it ended we would go our separate ways."

"I didn't agree to anything."

"Yes, *you* did," she retorted.

"No, I didn't," Myles argued softly. "When I asked you what happens at the end of the summer, you were the one who said 'we go our separate ways to live our separate lives.' And when I asked why you'd selected me to be your sex toy, your claim was 'we have a history.' Now, that doesn't sound as if I agreed to anything."

"Do you remember everything I say?"

"If it's worth remembering, then the answer is yes. I'm going to ask you again. Where do you see our relationship going? Do you want to stop at the end of the summer?"

Zabrina's mind was a tumult of confusion. What did he expect her to say? *Yes, I want it to continue beyond the summer because I'm still in love with you.* But had he thought about the three-hundred-mile separation? She lived in Philadelphia while he wanted to put down roots in Pittsburgh. Then she thought about Adam. How would he react to seeing his mother with another man when he was still dealing with the loss of his father and grandfather? The family therapist said Adam was progressing well, and it was she who suggested he spend time away from his mother because Zabrina had begun to mollycoddle a boy who was naturally independent.

The therapy sessions were good for her, too, because Zabrina realized she had several unresolved issues going back to her loss of her own mother. She somehow blamed herself for Isaac not remarrying and her childhood fixation with Myles Eaton would've been very unhealthy if he'd opted to take advantage of her infatuation.

"No, Myles, I don't want it to stop at the end of the summer. But what—"

Myles held up a hand, stopping her words. "Let it be, Brina," he warned in a quiet tone. "We'll let everything unfold naturally."

"Request permission to ask one more question, Professor Eaton."

Shaking his head, Myles couldn't help smiling. "What is it, Nurse Mixon?"

It was Zabrina's turn to smile, remembering when she'd passed her nursing boards and Myles had teased her, calling her Nurse Mixon. The smile faded as she formed the question she knew would answer whether she could ever hope for or consider a future with the man who'd unknowingly given her a piece of himself she would love forever.

"Do you love me, Myles?"

The seconds ticked off as swollen silence wrapped around them like a shroud, shutting out anything and everything around them. The waiting sent Zabrina's pulse spinning, her mind a maelstrom of anticipation and dread. Myles's withering gaze pinned her to her seat like a specimen under glass that would remain preserved in its natural state for posterity. Even if she lived to be a hundred she would never forget the look in his eyes.

"Yes, I love you, Zabrina." The admission came from somewhere so alien to Myles he couldn't begin to fathom where. "I've loved you for so long that I can't remember when I didn't love you. Even when you became another man's wife I loved you. When you opened your legs for him I still loved you. When you gave him the son that should've been ours I continued to love you. And, despite your sweet deception, I don't want you ever to question my feelings for you." He paused. "Have I made myself clear?"

Blinking back tears of joy, Zabrina nodded. "Yes."

The stone that had weighed down her heart the day Thomas Cooper had walked into her home to blackmail her into marrying a man who held her father's fate in his hands was rolled away with Myles's declaration of love.

She was freed from the threats when Thomas had fallen overboard and drowned in the Chesapeake. But her feelings then paled in comparison to those now that she was being given a second chance at love.

Myles hadn't mentioned marriage, and at thirty-three that wasn't as important to Zabrina as it had been when she was younger. Her mantra of 'enjoy what you have because when it ends you make certain you have no regrets' came to mind.

Pushing back his chair, Myles stood up, signaled the waiter and dropped several large bills on the table. "The food and service was excellent."

The waiter inclined his head. "Thank you, sir. Please come again."

Zabrina looked at Myles as if he'd taken leave of his senses. They'd just sat down to eat and he was leaving. Waiting until they were in the restaurant's parking lot, she rounded on him.

"What was that all about back there? You drive all the way from Philadelphia to Baltimore to eat and then we leave before we finish our dinner."

Myles assisted Zabrina up into the sport-utility vehicle. "We can eat at home."

She caught his meaning immediately. "Oh, really."

He flashed a Cheshire-cat grin. "Yes, really. We can cook together."

"Before we go to bed, or in bed?"

Myles leaned closer. "Both." He shut the door with a solid slam, rounded the vehicle and slid behind the wheel.

Although he'd never been much of a gambler, this time he had gambled *and* won. He knew he couldn't continue to sleep with Zabrina and not know where their relationship was going. If she'd been any other woman Myles would've been more than willing to have a summer fling, then move on from there. But they'd shared too much, and there was too much history between them for him to relegate her to the faceless, nameless women with whom he'd shared forgetful minutes of passion.

Myles completed the hundred-mile drive between Baltimore and Philadelphia in record time, maneuvering into Zabrina's driveway. She wanted him to stop at her house first. He'd just cut off the engine when Rachel came racing across the lawn, arms waving excitedly.

Zabrina removed her seat belt. "Do you want to wait here, or come in with me?" she asked Myles.

He lowered the driver's-side window, opened the door and came around to assist her down. "I'll wait on the porch for you." Cradling her face between his hands, he kissed her forehead. "Don't rush. I know how you ladies love to chat."

Zabrina pursed her lips in a provocative way that stirred the flesh between his legs. He chided himself for telling her not to rush. If Rachel hadn't come over, Myles would've gone inside with Zabrina and made love to her without the benefit of protection. If she were to become pregnant he would become her husband, not a baby daddy.

Too many women were raising children in households without fathers. His nieces, who had lost both parents in a horrific automobile accident, had been legally adopted by their aunt and uncle. They were luckier than some children who would've become a statistic in the foster-care system.

Zabrina's neighbor was a war widow, leaving her to

grieve the loss of her husband and the father of her young children. Zabrina had lost her father and husband within months of each other, leaving her son to grieve the loss of his father and grandfather. There had been too many losses, too much grief, especially for young children.

"Hi, Myles," Rachel called out as she mounted the porch.

"Hi, Rachel," he mimicked. "Bye, Rachel," he teased as she opened the door and went inside.

Chuckling to himself, he sat on the rocker and waited for Zabrina.

Rachel followed Zabrina into her bathroom, watching as she opened a drawer under the vanity. "I have a date," she said in a breathless whisper.

Zabrina turned and stared at her neighbor. Rachel's face was flushed with high color, her eyes large and sparkling like amethysts. "Who is he?"

Rachel pressed her palms together in a prayerful gesture. "Hugh Ormond."

"The owner of Whispers?"

"The one and only."

Zabrina screamed while jumping up and down like a hysterical teenager. She hugged Rachel, both of them doing the happy dance. "Yes, yes, yes!" she chanted. "I'm so happy for you. When did all of this happen?"

Rachel flashed a toothy grin. "He called me yesterday."

"How did he get your number?"

"Remember when he gave me his business card with his cell number?" Zabrina nodded. "Well, I called to make a reservation for my parents. I want to treat them to a night out for looking after Shane and Maggie, but the call went directly to voice mail. I left a message, asking him to return the call. When he finally called me back we ended up talking for an hour. He said he wanted to talk more, but he had to prepare for a private party. That's when he asked if I'd be willing to go out with him, and, of course, I said yes, but only after I played a little hard to get. I can't have him think I'm desperate, which I am."

Zabrina felt her neighbor's excitement. "When are you going out?"

"Tomorrow night. Please don't say anything to Myles that I'm seeing his friend."

"Why would I say anything to him?"

"I just don't want to jinx myself, Zabrina. This is not the first time a man has asked to go out with me, but it is the first time I've accepted. There was something about the others that gave me the willies." Rachel paused to take a breath. "Hugh is different because I feel so comfortable talking to him—about anything. I know my reluctance to date is because of my kids. I don't want Shane or Maggie to think I'm trying to replace their father with another man."

Zabrina offered Rachel a comforting smile. "You're a young woman and you're entitled to adult male companionship. And by that I don't necessarily mean sex."

Rachel blushed again. "But I want *and* need the sex, Zabrina. My husband and I used to screw like rabbits."

"Whoa, Rachel, that's entirely too much information."

The blonde rolled her eyes. "When you've been without a man for as long as I have you're ready to post a sign on your back reading, Man Wanted." She wrinkled her nose. "The only thing I've never been able to get into is online dating. Now that's some scary mess."

"I hear you," Zabrina agreed, not telling Rachel that it'd

been longer for her, before she starting sleeping with Myles again, since she'd been made love to.

Other than trolling clubs, she wouldn't know where to begin looking for a man. Fortunately, the only man she'd always loved had come back into her life when she least expected it.

She and Myles had put their past behind them in an attempt to move forward. However, one hurdle remained: their son. Zabrina knew Myles would eventually meet Adam when he returned from Virginia, but her uneasiness came from whether Adam would be willing to share his mother with a stranger.

"How are things going between you and Myles?"

Rachel's unexpected query pulled Zabrina from her reverie. She wanted to pretend she didn't know what her friend was talking about but knew it was futile. After all, she hadn't slept under her own roof in a couple of nights and her car hadn't been moved in days.

Resting a hip against the vanity she gave Rachel a long, penetrating stare. "Things are good."

Nervously, Rachel moistened her lips. "I know who you are," she said cryptically. "I know you're Senator Cooper's widow and that you were once engaged to Myles Eaton."

Zabrina's expression revealed none of what she was feeling at that moment: panic. She'd moved into her new home in mid-March and it was now the first week in July and not once in three months had Rachel given any indication that she knew who she was.

"How did you find out about me?"

"When you introduced me to Myles Eaton, I tried to recall where I'd heard his name. I searched the Internet and came up with quite a bit of information," she rambled on.

"And I know you ended your engagement to Myles and then married Thomas Cooper. Look, Zabrina, I know if you wanted me to know you would've told me. I would've asked but I was afraid you would've told me to mind my own business."

"How can I tell you to mind your business when my business is out there for everyone to read?" Zabrina asked. "I don't advertise who I am because I need to protect Adam. I've always tried to keep him out of the public eye, and so far I've succeeded."

Rachel pushed a smile through an expression of uncertainty. "Will you forgive me being nosy?"

"There's nothing to forgive." If anyone wanted to know about her, all they had to do was what Rachel had done—type her name into a search engine.

Flipping her ponytail over her shoulder, Rachel straightened to her full five-foot-nine-inch height. "I'm going to leave now, because I don't want your man mad at me for keeping you from him."

Zabrina exhaled a breath. She didn't want to be rude and tell her neighbor to go home, but Rachel tended to be Chatty Cathy. Wind her up and she'd talk for hours. And it was apparent Hugh Ormond liked her effervescent personality.

"I'll see you later," she said to Rachel.

"Later," Rachel repeated.

Waiting until her neighbor left, Zabrina gathered a supply of feminine products. Minutes later, she left the house to find Myles lounging on the rocker. He stood up as she closed and locked the door.

Myles wrapped an arm around Zabrina's waist as he led her off the porch. The day had begun with him waking up beside her and would end with her beside him. He didn't want to think of the day when he would have to return to Pittsburgh and not take her with him.

He'd lost her once because it was beyond his control. However, if it was within his control he did not intend to lose her a second time.

Chapter 13

Zabrina felt her heart rate kick into a higher gear as Myles maneuvered down the tree-lined street to the house where Belinda and Griffin Rice lived with their nieces. The newlyweds had returned from their honeymoon the week before and were now hosting their first get-together as husband and wife. In a matter of minutes she would come face-to-face with his parents, and interacting directly with Myles's parents wasn't something she was looking forward to.

She'd been surprised when Belinda called to invite her to Paoli for a time-honored Eaton Sunday dinner. Belinda said she'd already spoken to Myles, who'd offered to drive her. She'd declined previous invitations from Myles for her to share Sunday dinner with his mother and father, but Zabrina hadn't been able to form an appropriate excuse to get out of going to her childhood friend's house.

Since Adam was away, she'd changed her regular Sunday

routine. In the past she would prepare an elaborate dinner for the two of them, followed by driving to their favorite ice cream parlor for outrageous frozen concoctions. Now, after attending church services she drove over to Chinatown where she ate at a restaurant featuring Chinese and Thai cuisine. It was early evening when Myles came over and crawled into the hammock with her.

The past three weeks with Myles had been near-perfect, offering her a glimpse into what her life would've been like if they'd married. They went to bed, woke up, prepared meals and took long walks together. Afterward they spent hours in the hammock either sleeping or reading aloud to each other. It was as if time had stood still before Thomas Cooper had revealed her father's clandestine gambling addiction and theft of campaign funds, or as if she hadn't been blackmailed into breaking her engagement to Myles to marry her blackmailer.

Myles, slowing and downshifting, took a quick glance at Zabrina's delicate profile. He knew she'd clamped her teeth together by the throbbing muscle in her jaw. Belinda had called to inform him that she'd invited Zabrina to come to Paoli for a cookout and asked that he bring her. None of the Eatons knew he was sleeping with Zabrina and he wasn't going to volunteer the information because he didn't want a repeat of the exchange he'd had with Chandra.

He'd never interfered in his sisters' relationships and refused to tolerate any intrusion into his own. Myles had to admit he was somewhat surprised when Belinda informed him that she'd invited Zabrina to her wedding. It was something his sister said that made him rethink his attitude toward the woman to whom he'd given his heart: *Even after a criminal has served and completed his or her*

ten-year sentence society offers them a second chance.
Zabrina Mixon-Cooper wasn't a criminal, she hadn't
broken any law. The only thing she was guilty of was
breaking his heart.

Reaching over, he placed his hand over hers. Her fingers
were ice-cold. "Are you all right?"

Zabrina managed a tight smile. "I'm good."

Myles shot her another quick glance. "Your hands
are freezing."

"Cold hands, warm heart," she quipped, smiling.

Executing a smooth left turn, he maneuvered into a wide
driveway behind a gleaming black Volvo. "My folks are here."

Zabrina swallowed to relieve the dryness in her suddenly constricted throat. She didn't know what to expect
from Dwight and Roberta Eaton, but she doubted whether
they'd greet her as if she were a long-lost relative.

Symbolically, Roberta had become her surrogate
mother before and after Zabrina's mother passed away.
Whenever she slept over at the Eaton's large farmhouse-
style home she was treated the same as the other Eaton
siblings. Miss Bertie checked her hands for cleanliness
before she sat down to eat and Miss Bertie braided her hair,
always making certain the center part was straight. Bertie
used to say that whenever she saw a little girl with a
crooked part she felt compelled to pull the child aside and
redo her hair.

She waited for Myles to come around and help her
down. "Don't forget the flowers and gelato." Zabrina had
urged him to stop so she could purchase a bouquet of
flowers for the Rices' table and half pints of pistachio,
chocolate-hazelnut, peach and caffe latte gelato, packed in
a special container to keep them from melting. The day

before he'd had a case of assorted wine and a box of sliced rib-eye steaks delivered to Paoli after Belinda mentioned they were going to break with tradition and dine alfresco.

Griffin and Belinda's house reminded Zabrina of the one her friend had grown up in. Stately maple and oak trees provided shade for the white vinyl-sided three-story house with black shutters. The smell of grilling meat wafted in the air.

Cradling the foam crate of ice cream and the flowers in one hand, Myles cupped Zabrina's elbow with the other. "They're probably out back."

Zabrina hadn't realized she was holding her breath until she experienced tightness in her chest and was forced to exhale. A pair of sunglasses shielded her gaze as she stared at Layla and Sabrina Rice splashing in the inground pool under the watchful gaze of Belinda's parents.

Griffin stood at the stove in an outdoor kitchen, grilling franks. His wife, wearing an apron with The Real Cook stamped on the bib, filled tall glasses from a pitcher filled with lemon and lime slices floating in a pale yellow liquid.

Layla, floating on her back, spotted her uncle first. "Uncle Myles is here!"

Belinda turned, frowning at her niece. "Layla, there's no need to shout," she admonished softly.

Zabrina saw everyone's gaze directed at her and Myles. When she realized he was still holding her arm, she eased it surreptitiously from his loose grip. No one, nothing moved. It was as if a frame of film was frozen in place.

It was Belinda who broke the spell when she wiped her hands on a towel. Arms outstretched, she walked over to her brother and kissed his cheek, then Zabrina's. "I'm glad you could make it, Brina."

Zabrina felt her anxiousness fading. "Thank you for inviting me. You look absolutely beautiful. Mrs. Rice." She pressed her cheek to Belinda's.

Married life agreed with Belinda Rice. The Caribbean sun had darkened her face to a rich milk-chocolate hue and her promise to eat and relax was evident because the hollows in her slender face were gone. With her relaxed hair pulled back in a ponytail, shorts, tank top, sandals and bare face she looked as young as her high-school students.

Belinda's smile was shy, demure. "Thank you. Once everyone has eaten, I'll take you on a tour of the house."

Myles handed his sister the bouquet of flowers. "Brina brought these for the table, and there's gelato in the cooler."

"Please give them to Mama. She's the expert when it comes to arranging flowers." Belinda handed off the cooler to Griffin. "Please put this in the freezer." The outdoor kitchen was fully functional with a stainless-steel stove, grill, refrigerator/freezer, built-in bar and sinks.

Myles walked over to his parents, leaned over to kiss his mother's cheek, handed her the cellophane-wrapped bouquet, then patted his father's shoulder in an affectionate gesture. "Brina came with me," he said, sotto voce. Extending a hand, he eased Roberta up from her chair.

Zabrina removed her glasses at Roberta and Dwight Eaton's approach. She'd exchanged nods of acknowledgment with the two at Belinda's wedding, but they hadn't spoken to one another. She extended her hand to Roberta. "It's so nice seeing you again."

Roberta ignored her hand to hug her, surprising Zabrina with the unexpected display of affection. "How are you feeling, child?"

Zabrina went still, then relaxed as she returned the hug.

Had news gotten around that she'd had too much to drink at Belinda's wedding? "I'm well, Miss Bertie."

Roberta pulled back, staring up at the woman who'd made her only son's life a living hell. She'd wanted to hate the young woman who had deceived Myles, but couldn't. Zabrina was the daughter of a woman who'd died much too young, the best friend of her middle daughter, and someone whom she'd come to think of as her own daughter and the young woman who'd gotten Myles to fall in love with her when other women had tried and failed.

"You look very nice with short hair."

Zabrina, smiling, angled her head. "Thank you." She knew Roberta was looking for a crooked part, but she'd brushed her hair and kept it off her face and forehead with a candy-striped headband.

Roberta hadn't changed much. Her stylishly coiffed hair claimed more salt than pepper, and, although she'd added a few inches to her hips, she was still a very attractive middle-aged woman who'd been married to the same man for forty-two years.

Dr. Dwight Eaton came over to join them, his eyes warm, friendly behind a pair of rimless glasses. He, too, hugged Zabrina. It wasn't often that she saw the family doctor without his white shirt, tie and lab coat. Today he wore a golf shirt, khakis and slip-ons. A pager and two cell phones, devices that were essential to his profession, were attached to his belt.

"I didn't get a chance to talk to you at Lindy's wedding, but I wanted to tell you that I'm sorry for your loss. Isaac was truly a wonderful human being."

You wouldn't say that if you'd known he was a thief. Despite Thomas's accusations, Zabrina had never stopped loving her father. In fact, she loved him more because of his weakness. Fortunately, he'd stopped gambling, claiming he'd gone cold turkey once he became aware that he was going to become a grandfather. He said he didn't want his grandson or granddaughter growing up with the stigma that their grandfather had spent time in prison.

She hadn't wanted to believe Isaac, because Zabrina was aware that a gambling addiction was one of the most difficult to break. But Isaac was being truthful. She continued to monitor his bank accounts and Thomas had transferred the responsibility of handling his financial affairs from Isaac to another aide.

"Thank you, Dr. Dwight."

In keeping with her father's wishes, there had been a private ceremony, followed by cremation, and his ashes had been scattered in the ocean. Surviving family members included Isaac's sister, her daughter, three grandchildren, Zabrina and Adam. Thomas was saved the pretense of mourning his father-in-law. He was in Asia with several members of Congress on a fact-finding mission.

Roberta rested a hand on Zabrina. "I wish Dwight and I could've been there for you and your son when you lost Thomas Cooper so soon after losing your father. By the way, where is your son?"

"Adam is spending the month in Virginia with my cousin's children."

"I know you must really miss him," Roberta crooned.

"I do," Zabrina admitted.

She missed Adam, but not as much as she had the first week. It took three days of her calling her cousin twice a day to find out if Adam was having a good time, or giving her a problem before her Aunt Holly offered a stern lecture about the risks of being an overprotective mother. Holly sounded so much like Adam's therapist that she told the retired schoolteacher to have Adam call her whenever he felt like talking. He called home every third day before tapering off to once a week. Her son was expected to return to Philadelphia next Sunday. He'd begun whining that he wanted to stay longer, but Zabrina reminded him that his cousins were scheduled to go to a sleepaway camp for the first two weeks of August to give their parents a break from children. She did promise Adam he could return to Virginia the following summer *and* go to camp with his cousins.

"Dad, the game is on!" Myles called across the patio.

Dwight pressed a kiss to his wife's cheek. "Excuse me, ladies." Turning on his heel, he rushed over to where Griffin had set a flat-screen television on a stand under the retractable awning shading the patio from the hot summer sun.

"Make certain you keep your eyes on your granddaughters, too, Dwight Eaton."

"I will, Bertie." Dwight shifted his chair where he could view the ball game and Sabrina and Layla.

"Come help me arrange your flowers, Brina. I don't understand these men and their obsession with a ball," she mumbled under her breath. "If it's not a golf ball, then it's baseball, basketball or football." Roberta's angry gaze met Zabrina's amused one. "What's up with the balls?"

Zabrina bit back a smile. "I don't know, Miss Bertie."

She remembered when Griffin, his brother Grant, Myles and Dwight would gather in the Eatons' family room to watch sporting events ranging from auto racing and bowling to soccer. If a ball was involved, then the men were armchair spectators.

The last time Zabrina had seen Layla and Sabrina Rice

they'd been toddlers, so it was a bit unsettling to see them as young adults. It reminded her how much time had passed and that Myles's nieces and Adam were cousins. She followed Roberta into an enclosed back porch to a large updated gourmet kitchen, watching as the older woman retrieved a vase and filled it with water.

Roberta opened the cellophane wrapping and picked up stems of lily of the valley, snow-white roses and hydrangea, sweet pea, peonies and baby's breath. "I hope you and Myles get it right this time." She glanced up from her task to find Zabrina staring at her. "You think I don't know what's going on between you and my son?"

"I suppose you don't approve?"

"It has nothing to do with whether I do or don't approve, Brina. You and Myles are grown, and once my children were adults I learned to bite my tongue and keep my opinions to myself."

"I'm sorry—"

Roberta held up a hand. "Don't go there, Zabrina. Whatever happened between you and Myles is in the past. What's more important is the future. I know you love him, and that he loves you. That was very apparent when he couldn't stop staring at you at Lindy's wedding. You're luckier than most women, young lady, because you've been offered a second chance with a man you love."

"You…you believe Myles still loves me?" Zabrina had asked Roberta the question despite knowing the answer. He'd been forthcoming when he'd told her he loved her— in and out of bed.

"Myles never stopped loving you, Brina. No, he didn't tell me but I know my children a lot better than they believe I do. The back and forth between Griffin and Belinda was nothing more than 'I like you but I'm not going to let you know it.' Unfortunately it took a family tragedy for them to come together for the sake of my grandchildren. Griffin has shown that he can be a great father and Belinda is a wonderful mother." Roberta flashed a wide smile. "They've promised me that they're doing their best to give Dwight and me more grandchildren. Dwight wants a grandson, but I'm open to either a girl or boy."

Zabrina wanted to tell Roberta that she and Dwight had a grandson. Adam Cooper was their grandson. She'd mentally rehearsed how she would eventually tell Myles that Adam was his. She owed it to him and to Adam to let them know their biological connection. She'd sworn that she would never divulge the circumstances of her marriage to Thomas, but she hadn't sworn or promised anyone that she wouldn't tell Myles that he'd fathered her child. She knew she couldn't go back and right the wrongs, but she wanted to make certain to make sure things were right.

Adam had a right to know why Thomas had been so distant, why he wasn't or couldn't be the traditional father and why Isaac Mixon did all the things with him Thomas should've done.

And Myles had a right to know that he was a father and that he could share all the things with Adam he'd talked about when they were engaged. Myles, at twenty-eight, had wanted to start a family right away, while she'd wanted to wait, not because she'd wanted an extended honeymoon but because of a repressed fear that her life would duplicate her mother's, that she wouldn't live to see her child reach his or her majority.

"I love Myles, Miss Bertie. Even when I was another man's wife I still loved him. Some people would say I was an adulterer, but I really don't care. I never wished Thomas Cooper ill and I'm not ashamed to say I never shed a tear when the police told me he'd drowned, nor at his funeral."

Lines of concern furrowed Roberta's forehead. "What did he do to you, Brina?"

Without warning, her maternal instincts had surfaced. She'd come to love Zabrina Mixon as if she were a daughter after she'd lost her mother. Although she was raising four rambunctious children who insisted on bringing animals into her house, she'd welcomed Zabrina with open arms, because her rationale was, what was one more child at her table?

"He didn't do anything to me, Miss Bertie, that I hadn't permitted him to do."

"Had he harmed or posed a threat to your son?"

Zabrina's expression changed, her face suddenly grim. "No. And if he had I wouldn't have stayed with him. I don't know what's going to happen with me and Myles beyond the summer, but we'll probably remain friends."

Roberta gave her son's girlfriend a skeptical glance as she sucked her teeth. "Friends? Don't delude yourself, Brina. You and Myles haven't been friends in a very long time."

She knew she'd shocked Zabrina when her mouth opened but no words came out. Only someone visually impaired didn't see the tenderness in Myles's eyes whenever he looked at Zabrina. When they'd walked onto the patio Roberta hadn't missed how protectively Myles held on to Zabrina's arm. It was as if he had to hold on to her to make certain she wouldn't get away from him.

She also noticed something very different about Myles that hadn't been apparent when he'd returned to Philadelphia years ago, trips that were too short and infrequent. She knew he was aware that Zabrina was now a widow, and once Belinda told him that she'd invited Zabrina to her wedding Myles spoke of a possible extended stay in Philly. This revelation shocked everyone—everyone except his mother. She knew if anyone could get Myles Eaton to spend more than a week in Philly it was Zabrina Cooper.

"You're right, Miss Bertie. Myles and I are sleeping together."

"Good." She placed the bouquet in the vase, and stood back to admire her handiwork. "Now, maybe you'll give me a grandchild, too."

"Who's going to give you a grandchild?"

Roberta and Zabrina turned to find Myles leaning against the entrance to the kitchen, muscular arms crossed over his broad chest. "Well, ladies? What's up?"

Roberta spoke first. "Why are you eavesdropping on a private conversation?"

Taking long strides, Myles walked into the kitchen. "I wasn't eavesdropping. I got here in time to hear the word *grandchild*."

"Your mother said she wants more grandchildren," Zabrina volunteered.

Myles lifted an eyebrow. "Bertie Eaton can speak for herself, Brina."

Pinpoints of heat dotted Zabrina's cheeks at his retort. Her eyes narrowed, reminding him of a cat about to pounce. "I'm more than aware of that, Myles Eaton."

Roberta recognized the tension between her son and Zabrina. It was palpable. Normally she wouldn't interfere in the scraps between her children and their partners, but she wasn't going to stand by and let Myles intimidate the woman who'd suffered too many losses in her young life.

"And you need to watch your tone, Myles Adam Eaton."

Myles gave his mother an incredulous look before his eyes narrowed. "What did I say?"

Roberta rested her hands on her hips, a gesture her children easily recognized. It meant she'd had enough and it was better that they walk away than stand and debate with her. "It's not what you say, but how you said what you said."

Myles threw up his hands. "How did I say it!?"

"What's going on in here, Mama?" Belinda had walked into the kitchen. "And, Myles, why are you raising your voice?"

Knowing when he was bested, Myles threw up his hands again, this time in defeat. "Women," he whispered under his breath.

Roberta cupped a hand to her ear. "You got a problem with the so-called weaker sex?"

Mumbling an expletive, Myles walked out of the kitchen to the sound of hysterical female laughter. Belinda had sent him to get Zabrina, and he'd reached the kitchen in time to hear his mother mention a grandchild. Roberta had talked about having more grandchildren after he'd proposed to Zabrina because Donna and Grant Rice had decided beforehand that they wanted two children, but hadn't counted on getting two at the same time.

Reaching for a napkin, Belinda blotted the tears filling her eyes. "That wasn't nice, Mama."

Roberta waved a hand. "It serves him right. There are times when Myles is full of himself. I've told him that with his attitude he should be sitting on the bench instead of teaching law."

"Judge Eaton," Belinda crooned. "I kinda like the sound of that. What do you think, Brina?"

Zabrina smiled. "It sounds good to me, too."

Picking up the vase of flowers, Belinda cradled it to her chest. "If Myles is appointed judge and you marry him, Brina, then I'll have to address your mail to the Honorable Judge Myles and Zabrina Eaton."

"I'm not marrying Myles." The protest was out of Zabrina's mouth before she could censor herself.

Wincing, Belinda bit her lip. "I'm sorry, Brina. I didn't—"

"Please don't apologize, Lindy. Myles and I are just hanging out together for the summer." For Zabrina, sleeping together didn't necessary lead to a marriage proposal, or a promise of happy ever after.

Belinda blew out a breath. "Now that I've taken my foot out of my mouth I'll take these outside. By the way, I sent Myles in to get you because he's offered to make Philly cheese steaks."

Zabrina's eyes lit up. "Is he using Cheez Whiz or provolone?"

"Please," Belinda drawled. "It's a sacrilege not to go with the Whiz."

"Even though Dwight told me I should watch my cholesterol, I'm going to have a bite of his," Roberta said.

Belinda shot her mother a pointed look. "Now, Mama, you know that Daddy's not going to let you take a bite of his Philly cheese with Whiz," she teased with the right amount of South Philly *atty-tood*. Regulars and tourists who lined up at Pat's or Gino's were familiar with the debate as to which sandwich was better: Cheez Whiz or provolone, *wit'* or *wit'out,* which translated into with or without onions. "We'll snack until the game is over," she continued, "then we'll sit down to eat dinner."

Zabrina wanted to tell Belinda she would eat dinner only *if* she wasn't too full. Somehow she'd forgotten the amount of food the Eatons consumed on Sunday afternoons. What she found surprising was that none of them had a weight problem.

She followed mother and daughter out of the kitchen to the rear of the house where the aroma of steak filled the air. Myles had taken over the grilling duties, chopping the thinly sliced steak as though he performed the task every day. A pot of Cheez Whiz sat on a back burner over a low flame. Griffin and Dwight, sitting on chairs while holding bottles of cold beer, groaned in unison when the Phillies pitcher gave up another run.

Accepting a glass of lemonade from Belinda, Zabrina put on her sunglasses, lay down on a cushioned lounger and closed her eyes. She'd applied a layer of the highest number sunblock to her face and arms. Reuniting with the Eatons had gone more smoothly than she'd anticipated. But, then again, ten years was a very long time to hold on to a grudge.

She knew firsthand how hate festered until it eventually destroyed its host. It was only when she'd unconsciously forgiven Thomas Cooper that she'd begun to experience a modicum of peace.

Life was good. She'd rediscovered love and passion with Myles Eaton, and she would reunite with her son in exactly one week. Her only concern was how Adam would react when she introduced him to his biological father for the first time.

Chapter 14

Zabrina kept pace with Myles and the real estate agent as the silver-haired, fashionably dressed woman gave them a tour of a house that had just come on the market.

The call had come in on Myles's cell phone before seven that morning. He'd joined her in the shower, announcing he had to return to Pittsburgh before noon and he wanted her to come along. It wasn't until they were an hour into the drive that he revealed his Realtor wanted to show him a house that met his specifications. The Realtor had downloaded pictures of the house to Myles's BlackBerry, and he was anxious to see it in person.

The house, all fifty-five hundred square feet of it, was magnificent. The sixty-year-old structure was erected on three acres overlooking a valley ten miles outside Pittsburgh. It had everything Myles wanted: wraparound porch, fireplaces in each of the four bedrooms, four full baths, two half baths, entry hall, great room, living and formal dining rooms, three-car garage and screened back porch. The former owners had put the house up for sale and moved into a retirement community when it became impossible for them to maintain, and their children preferred condo living to mowing lawns and shoveling snow.

Mrs. Eck smiled at Myles. "I have documentation verifying the plumbing and electricity were updated two years ago."

Reaching for Zabrina's hand, Myles cradled it in the crook of his arm. "If I decide to purchase the house, then I'll hire my own engineer to check out everything."

"Mrs. Eaton, you also might want to update the kitchen appliances. That is, if you and your husband agree you want the house. Do you have children, Mrs. Eaton?"

Zabrina hesitated, while at the same time staring at Myles. He nodded. "Yes. We have a son." The admission had slipped out unbidden, but Myles didn't appear to notice her damning faux pas.

The petite woman with sapphire-blue eyes clapped her hands. "Wonderful. Come out back with me and I'll show you what the former owners erected for their grandsons."

Myles covered the hand tucked into his elbow as he followed Mrs. Eck across the kitchen and out a set of French doors to the backyard. He wanted the house. He'd wanted it even before seeing inside.

The smile that began with his mouth tilting at the corners spread to his eyes. Someone had built a miniature log cabin that doubled as a playhouse. The other surprise was a ladder attached to the trunk of a massive maple tree that led up to a large tree house. He hadn't met Zabrina's son, but he had no doubt the young boy would love spending time in the tree house or hanging out in the cabin.

"Do you think Adam would like it?"

Zabrina could hear her heart echoing in her ears. Myles was answering a question to which he knew the answer. *Their* son would love the tree house. She knew if she couldn't find Adam in the house then he would be either in the tree house or the log cabin daydreaming about the alternate universes he created in his fertile imagination that eventually came to life on paper.

"He would love it."

"How about Adam's mother? Does she like the house?"

Zabrina felt as if she'd been frozen for more than a decade and had begun to thaw. She couldn't remember when she hadn't been in love with Myles Eaton, and if she'd doubted her feelings, she knew now for certain that she was hopelessly and inexorably in love with him.

"Adam's mother loves the house."

A sense of strength and peace came to Zabrina with the pronouncement. She'd made her feelings for Myles known to him, his mother, his sister, and the only person that remained was *their* son.

Myles met the Realtor's hopeful expression with a warm smile. "If you'll allow me a few minutes, I'd like to talk to *Mrs. Eaton.*"

"Take all the time you need, Professor Eaton."

After waiting until Mrs. Eck returned to the house, Myles cradled Zabrina's face in his hands. The rain blanketing the western part of the state had stopped, but one-hundred-percent humidity had frizzed her short hair.

"Do you like it, darling?"

Zabrina's eyelids fluttered wildly. "It shouldn't be whether I like it, Myles. The question is do *you* like it."

He nodded. "I love the house, I love you, and I want you and Adam to live here with me."

She stared at a tiny bird perched on the branch of a sapling. "I can't live with you, Myles."

"I thought you said you loved me."

Her gaze shifted to his mouth, bracketed with lines of tension. "I do love you."

"Then why won't you live with me?"

"If I didn't have Adam I would do it in a heartbeat. But what message would I send him if I shack up with a man who's not my husband? I thought sending him to a private school would shield him from kids whose mothers expose their children to a revolving door of men who come and go at will. One month there's Uncle Bobby, then six months later there's Uncle Jimmy. After a while the names and faces become a jumble. Some of them slept with the same men just to compare notes."

"How did you find out about his classmates' mothers' sexcapades?"

"Adam slept over at a friend's house and he heard someone call the mother a name. He came home and asked me what a ho meant."

"And you told him?"

"Of course I did, Myles."

Wrapping his arms around her waist, Myles molded her to his length. "You think if you move here with me Adam will think badly of you?"

"Yes."

"If you married me would you still be a ho?"

Zabrina could feel Myles's heart thudding against her

own. She realized he was as apprehensive about marrying as she was. "Are…are you proposing marriage?"

"No, Brina. I'm *asking* you to marry me."

"Again?"

He smiled and attractive lines fanned out around his eyes. "Yes—again."

She still hadn't processed what she was hearing. "You want me to marry you because you want me to live in this house with you?"

Hard-pressed not to shake her until her teeth rattled, Myles clenched his own teeth to stop the curses poised on the tip of his tongue. "The house has nothing to do with it, Zabrina." He angled his head and brushed a light kiss over her parted lips. "You said there were no do-overs in life, but you're so wrong, Brina. Call it luck, fate, providence or destiny, but we've been given a second chance.

"I don't know, nor do I care why you married Thomas Cooper. What matters is you're free to marry whomever you want. If you don't want to marry me, then I need to know now before I get in any deeper. And if you say no, then I'll drive you back to Philly and I'll never bother you again. That's not a promise, Zabrina. That's a vow."

Zabrina saw the torture in the eyes of the man she'd once promised to marry. She'd deceived him once and he'd taken her back. Fate had given her a second chance and all she had to do was open her mouth and say yes. *Yes, I will marry you, Myles Eaton. Yes I will move to Pittsburgh and live in what will become our dream house. Yes I will share everything I have, and that includes your son.*

"Yes," she whispered, the word coming from a place she hadn't known existed.

Myles's dark eyes riveted her to the spot. "Yes what, Zabrina?"

"Yes, Myles, I will marry you."

"Will you and Adam live here with me?"

This was the side of Myles that irked Zabrina. "What if I tell you that I want you to move in with me and Adam?"

"Then, I'd do it! I would move anywhere, Zabrina. Anywhere as long as it is with you."

She hesitated before giving him an answer. Zabrina knew Myles wanted the house, wanted it as much as he wanted to marry her, yet he'd give it up for her. She shook her head as tears pricked the backs of her lids. "If anyone's going to do any moving it will be me and Adam."

One moment she was standing and within the next Zabrina found herself swept off her feet as Myles swung her around and around, shouting at the top of his lungs. He was going to get everything he'd ever wanted: Zabrina, a son and their dream house.

"We'll get married as soon as we get back to Philly unless…"

"Unless what, Myles?"

He set her on her feet. "Unless we fly to Vegas, get married, then come back and have a little something for the family once you decorate the house however you want it."

"No. No," she repeated. "I can't do that to Adam."

"Do what?"

"Introduce you as my husband and his new dad the first time he meets you. I'm not saying I need his approval, but it's only fair that the two of you spend some time together before we all live under the same roof."

Myles ran a hand over his face. "You're right, baby. I'm sorry." His lips came down to meet hers in a dreamy intimacy that felt both trembling. "Let's go inside and tell Mrs. Eck that she can start counting her commission."

Zabrina wasn't certain whether she'd be able to sell her house, and if she couldn't then she'd rent it. She was sorry to leave Rachel and her children, but if her soon-to-be ex-neighbor wanted to come to Pittsburgh to visit, she and Myles had plenty of room to put them up.

"This is where I live, darling."

Zabrina walked around Myles's furnished apartment in what once had been a small hotel. He told her he'd turned down an offer for faculty housing because he valued his privacy. The accommodations were less than opulent, but serviceable and within walking distance of the law-school campus.

The apartment had a miniscule bedroom, a bathroom with a shower stall, basin and commode and a utility kitchen with a dining area. Everything was in its place, but somehow it still looked cramped to her. Myles stacked law books on the floor along one wall of the bedroom because he said there was no room for a bookcase.

"Do you mind if I open the windows, Myles?"

"Of course not." The windows hadn't been opened since he'd left a month ago.

Zabrina opened the windows overlooking the front of the two-story building. Now that she saw for herself the size of the apartment she realized why he'd wanted a lot more space. A futon doubled as a sofa in what passed for the living room.

They'd driven back to the real estate office with the agent, where Myles signed countless documents, then wrote a check for the down payment. Mrs. Eck told him that because he'd been preapproved he could expect to close on the property the third week in August. That would give him time to settle in before classes began.

The heat from Myles's body seeped into hers when he came to stand behind her. "What are you thinking about, Brina?"

"I'm thinking about going back to work."

"Why?"

"I miss nursing. I've managed to take some continuing education courses to stay current, but it's not the same."

Myles wrapped his arms around her waist. He pressed his face to her damp hair. "What about Adam?"

"What about him, Myles?"

"Who's going to watch him when you're working?"

Zabrina closed her eyes. "I'm going to go online and see if there are any school-nurse positions available. That way our hours will be the same."

Myles nuzzled the side of her neck. "We could hire a housekeeper who could also double as sitter."

"Let me check the employment possibilities first."

"Whatever you decide, Brina, I'll back you up."

How different her marriage to Myles would be from the one she'd had with Thomas Cooper. The time she'd broached the subject of going back to the hospital Thomas had reacted like a mad man. He claimed the wife of an important politician shouldn't be seen emptying bedpans, saying it was bad for his image. The following day her father had come to Cooper Hall to talk to her. When he'd told her that she shouldn't do or say anything to upset Thomas, she'd asked Isaac to leave. The look on her father's face was one she would remember all her days. Whenever Thomas couldn't get her to agree to something, he enlisted her father's assistance. And she knew if Isaac hadn't done his son-in-law's bidding, he would be reminded of the threat of going to jail.

Staring up at Myles over her shoulder, she blew him a kiss. "Thank you, darling."

"You're welcome. What do you think of my humble abode?" he whispered in her ear.

"It's very, very humble."

"Damn, baby, you didn't have to say it like that."

She giggled. "What did you expect me to say? That it's Buckingham Palace?"

"It's *my* palace—at least temporarily."

"True."

"Have you seen the royal bedchamber?"

Resting the back of her head on his shoulder, Zabrina closed her eyes. "I thought I caught a glimpse of it."

"Would you like to take a tour?"

Turning in his embrace, she stared up at Myles, stunned at what she saw in his dark eyes. Her whole body trembled from a need so great she felt as if she were coming out of her skin.

"I want you to make love to me."

The last word wasn't off her tongue when Myles swept Zabrina up in his arms and carried her into the bedroom. What happened next was a blur. Within minutes of him placing her on the bed, her clothes lay on the floor with his.

The blood had rushed to his penis so quickly he felt light-headed. Lowering himself he smothered her mouth with his, pushing into her body with one sure thrust of his hips. Her smell, her moist heat and the way her flesh fitted around his sent him over the edge. The rush of completion came so quickly that he pulled out and slid down the length of her body.

Bracing both hands on her inner thighs, he spread Zabrina's legs apart and feasted like a starving man. His rapacious tongue was unrelenting and uncompromising. He heard her screaming for him to stop, but he continued his sensual assault. It was when she arched off the mattress that he knew he'd brought her maximum pleasure.

Zabrina moaned softly when Myles moved over her languid body, gasping sharply when he entered her with a force that rekindled her waning passion all over again. At the moment his breathing quickened, she managed to slip out from under his bucking body. The sudden motion surprised Myles and he sat up, giving her the advantage she needed to take him into her mouth.

It was the first time she'd gone down on Myles and now she knew why he liked it. The position was one of power *and* control. Grasping his penis, she held it tightly as her tongue went up one side and then down the other as if she were licking a frothy confection.

A sense of strength came to her when he howled, flailed his arms and begged her to stop. Zabrina had no intention of stopping—not until he yielded to the pleasure he sought to withhold from her.

"Baby, baby, please baby, no," he chanted. It began as a litany that resounded in her head, and still she wouldn't relent.

Myles knew he had to extricate Zabrina's mouth before he ejaculated. He went completely still and when her head came up he moved quickly. Flipping her onto her back, he went to his knees, raised her legs in the air and entered her again. The turbulence of their passion knew no bounds when they shuddered simultaneously in a shared ecstasy that left both trembling.

Zabrina found herself crying and babbling incoherently as Myles lay down next to her. He held her as if she were a child until she quieted and drifted off to sleep.

Zabrina woke to find herself in bed—alone. Pinpoints of fading light came through the blinds at the single window. She sat up, swung her legs over the side of the mattress, then she felt the sticky residue on her thighs. She and Myles had made love without protection! A low moan slipped from her when she realized she was ovulating. How, she bemoaned, could she have been so careless? The door to the bedroom opened and the outline of Myles's body filled the doorway.

He touched the dimmer switch on the wall and the small space was filled with light from the table lamp. Zabrina stared at him as if he were a stranger.

"Where are my clothes?"

"I put them in the wash."

"In the wash?"

Myles walked into the room. He'd changed out of his slacks and into a pair of faded jeans. "I have a portable washer/dryer in a closet off the kitchen." He made his way to a chest of drawers and took out a T-shirt. He handed it to her. "You can put that on if you want. Personally I wouldn't mind if you run around in the buff."

She took the T-shirt, but didn't put it on. "I need to take a shower. I smell like sex."

"Wrong, Brina. You smell like a woman who has been made love to."

"Very funny, Myles."

"Before you take a shower I'd like to give you something."

Zabrina watched as he searched in the bottom of a narrow closet. He went to his knees, cursing under his breath. "What are you cursing about?"

"I'm looking for something," came his muffled reply. "Got it!"

Zabrina felt her knees give way slightly before she maintained her balance when she saw what Myles cradled on the palm of his hand. It was the ring she'd returned to him via a bonded messenger.

He beckoned her closer. "Come here, baby."

Zabrina held her breath, unable to move. It *was* a do-over. For the second time Myles Eaton would slip an engagement ring on her finger. She extended her left hand, unable to control its shaking. The ring was one she and Myles had designed together: an exceptional two-carat fancy yellow diamond in a square-cut modern shape set off by a carat of trapezoids and another carat of round diamonds in a platinum setting. The jeweler had said he was giving them a discount on the price of the ring when he charged them for the loose stones and not the setting. The final price tag was staggering, but Myles said she was more than worth it.

He went to his knees in front of her. "Brina Mixon, will you do me the honor of becoming my wife?"

She thought about telling him that legally she was Zabrina Cooper, but she didn't want to spoil the very special moment. Their gazes met, fused as they shared a smile. "Yes, Myles Adam Eaton, I will marry you."

He slipped the ring on her left hand. Her finger was smaller than it'd been years before. Myles stood up.

Zabrina held up her hand to the light. "Even though it's a little big, it is still spectacular."

Reaching for her hand, Myles dropped a kiss on her knuckle. "This is where it belongs, and no matter what passes between us I don't ever want you to take it off again." Turning her hand over, he pressed a kiss on her palm. "I'm going to have to fatten you up some," he teased.

"If you continue to make love to me without protection you won't have to worry about fattening me up. In nine months I'll look as if I've swallowed a watermelon."

"I'm sorry, Brina. I don't know what happened."

Looping her arms under his shoulders, Zabrina pressed her bare breasts to his chest. "I'll know in another week or two whether you're going to give your mother that grandchild she wants."

"My mother has been harping about having more grandchildren for years now. I think it started when Donna and Grant said they were stopping after the twins were born."

"She's blessed, Myles. Layla and Sabrina are incredible granddaughters."

Zabrina found the girls shy around strangers, but once they had warmed to her it was as if she'd known them all their lives. When she'd told them that she had a son they offered to babysit, until she revealed that Adam was a ten-year-old.

The girls had been bright and engaging when Zabrina had joined them when they took Nigel and Cecil for a walk. They'd showed her their new school before they retraced their steps and joined the rest of the family for dinner on the patio. Zabrina marveled at how well-adjusted her son's cousins were, because it hadn't been a year since they'd lost both parents in a drunk-driving accident.

Belinda had revealed that the girls had been in counseling to work through their issues of death and loss. She would've continued with the sessions if the twins hadn't decided they didn't want to keep talking about their mother and father.

Zabrina knew there would come a time when Adam would want to stop seeing his counselor. He hadn't gone in four weeks and she was anxious to see if missing his sessions had impacted his emotional growth.

Tilting her chin, she smiled at Myles. "I think I'm going to take a shower now."

He lifted his eyebrows questioningly. "Do you want company?"

"No, Myles. The shower stall is too small for two people."

"No, it's not."

Her smile slipped away. The three words spoke volumes. While she'd been pining away for Myles Eaton she realized he hadn't been pining for her. How many women had he slept with since their breakup? And how many had he made love to on the same bed where he might possibly have gotten her pregnant for the second time?

"I have to take a shower." She tried walking around him, but he blocked her way. "Please let me go, Myles."

"Look at me, Brina. I said, look at me," he repeated when she stared at the floor. Her head came up. "Yes, I've slept with other women, and I'm not going to apologize for it. But I want you to know that I never cheated on you when we were together."

"And I've never cheated on you, Myles. Not ever!"

A frown appeared between his eyes when he realized what she'd said. "What are you talking about?"

"Adam. He's your son, not Thomas Cooper's. I was pregnant when I married Thomas."

Zabrina clenched her jaw to muffle the sobs building in

the back of her throat when she saw the tortured look in Myles's eyes. She'd planned to tell him that he was Adam's father, but she hadn't wanted it to come out like it did. She'd known however she told him it would be shocking *and* painful, however, the way Myles was glaring at her had chills pebbling her flesh.

"You're lying!" Myles said, after he recovered his voice. He wanted to believe Zabrina was lying, lashing out to wound him because she was jealous he'd admitted to sleeping with other women.

"No, Myles, I'm not lying."

"You couldn't have been pregnant because you were on the pill."

"Yes, I was on the pill. I was taking the lowest dose, and I was one of a small percentage of women who get pregnant while taking the pill."

Zabrina's explanation grated on Myles's nerves. His hands snaked around her upper arms, holding her captive. "Why didn't you tell me, Zabrina? Why did you allow another man to claim *my* son, give him *his* name instead of mine?"

"It's too complicated to explain."

Myles shook his head as if to clear it. He couldn't believe what Zabrina had just told him. She had to be lying, just like she'd lied when she'd told him that she was in love with another man. Who was she? Had he fallen in love with a pathological liar?

He dropped his hands as if he feared contamination and she lost her balance, falling backward. Reacting quickly, Myles caught Zabrina before she fell. She was shaking uncontrollably. Sweeping her up into his arms, he placed her on the bed, his body following hers down.

   Myles wanted answers, but more importantly he wanted
the truth, and if he had to hold Zabrina prisoner in the small
furnished apartment to get it he would do just that.

Chapter 15

"I was blackmailed into marrying Thomas Cooper."

The words burned the back of Zabrina's throat as they spilled off her tongue like bile. She'd sworn that she would never tell anyone how she'd come to marry Thomas, but she was tired, tired of lying and even more tired of hiding.

It was no longer about her or her father. Isaac Mixon was gone, impervious to the threats of a man obsessed with power. Thomas was gone and could no longer hurt her *or* her son.

She told Myles everything—leaving nothing out. She confessed to sharing a bed with Thomas on their wedding night without consummating their marriage. It was as if the floodgates were opened when she talked about the political photo-ops, how, after she gave birth, she withdrew from her social engagements and whenever she tried to exert her independence Thomas used Isaac as his enforcer *to keep her in her place.*

"He used fear and intimidation to control my father, and he knew I'd do anything to keep Daddy from going to jail."

Myles felt tightness in his chest before realizing he'd been holding his breath. He hadn't wanted to believe Zabrina, but there was no way she could make up a story so incredible and bizarre.

"Why didn't you tell me, Brina?"

"I couldn't," she whispered. "Thomas would've had someone kill my father." She told him about the man holding a gun to Isaac's head.

"No, he wouldn't. Your father was his trump and get-out-of-jail card and if he had Isaac murdered then it would've derailed his carefully orchestrated political career. Thomas couldn't marry his cousin's wife, so you became the pawn for a fortysomething bachelor who needed a wife to enhance his image, and Isaac delivered you like a trussed-up holiday bird. Adam was an added bonus he hadn't counted on."

"Adam carries his name, but Thomas hardly ever gave our son a passing glance."

Myles smiled for the first time since being told he'd fathered a child. Zabrina had said *our son.* He wanted to tell her Thomas ignoring the child wasn't a bad thing, because he planned to share things with Adam they should've shared years ago. It would also make it easier for him to step into the role of father because Adam wouldn't have to deal with guilt when he replaced one father figure with another.

"I'm sorry you had to sacrifice your happiness for your father's misdeeds and I'm sorry Adam had to spend the first ten years of his life with a monster who didn't have the decency to pretend to be a father."

Zabrina grasped the front of Myles's T-shirt. "You can't

tell Adam about his grandfather. It would crush him if he found out that Isaac stole money."

"Don't worry, baby. I won't say anything.

"If you hadn't waited ten years to tell me this I know I could've gotten your father off," he said after a comfortable silence.

"What are you talking about?"

"I would've taken on your father's case and because it was his first offense I would've asked the DA to give him probation. Then again, there could've been the possibility that the charges might have been thrown out."

Closing her eyes, Zabrina pressed her face to the side of Myles's neck. "I hadn't thought of that. How could I have been so stupid and gullible?"

"There wasn't much you could do with a gun pointed at your father's head."

"Yeah, but—"

"But nothing," he interrupted. "You couldn't risk trying to negotiate with a megalomaniac. There was still the possibility Cooper would've had someone hurt your father."

"But I should've trusted you, Myles, because you'd promised to protect me."

"Yes, I did promise. But you did what you did because you believed at that time it was best for your father and unborn child."

A beat passed. "Are you ready to meet your son? He's coming home Sunday."

"If I'm not ready, then I'll have to get ready."

"I'd like for us to wait a while before we tell Adam you're his biological father."

Myles kissed her hair. "I don't have a problem with that. It may be too much for him to take in right now."

"What about your family, Myles?"

"What about them, baby?"

"Are we going to tell them that Adam is an Eaton?"

Myles smiled down at the woman who'd sacrificed herself for her father. He didn't want to think of what she would do for their son. "We'll tell them after we legally change his name from Cooper to Eaton."

"Will he have to undergo a paternity test?"

"I doubt it, Brina. Cooper's dead so he can't contest it. I'm marrying Adam's mother, so it wouldn't be out of the ordinary that I'd adopt her child. Adam's actual paternity will remain an Eaton secret."

Zabrina reached up and traced the outline of Myles's expressive eyebrows with her forefinger. "When do you want to get married?"

"I'll leave that up to you. The last time we planned a wedding together I thought I was going to lose my mind. For this one I'm going to opt out of the planning. Let me know the date, time and place and I'll show up."

She gave him a soft punch to the shoulder, encountering solid muscle. "We don't have to rush and marry unless I find out I'm carrying another Eaton after that last stunt you pulled."

Myles held up his pinky. "No more unprotected lovemaking."

Zabrina looped her pinky with his. "No more unprotected lovemaking," she repeated.

"I'd like to make a few renovations to the house."

"What do you want?"

"I'd like to put in a home spa in the master bath. I also would like to redo the floors in the entry, kitchen and all of the bathrooms. Of course, the kitchen has to be re-modeled and—"

"Whoa, hold up, baby girl. How much of the interior do you want to change?"

Zabrina wrinkled her nose. "I'll have to go through each room with a decorator, and then I'll make my decision. And don't worry about the cost. I'll pay for it."

"No, Zabrina. I'll pay for the renovations."

"You will not, Myles Eaton. I made out quite well for the ten years I had to spend in captivity. When Thomas Cooper died, he left me very well off, and I would like nothing better than to spend the money decorating my new home where I'll live with my husband and children."

"Let's make a deal, baby. You take care of what goes on inside the house and I'll take care of what goes on outside."

"Like riding lawnmowers and snowblowers?"

"There you go. I think you're getting the hang of it."

"How about the tree and playhouse?"

"That, too."

"Hammocks?"

"Hot damn, baby girl. You're a quick learner."

"You forgot something, Myles."

"What's that?"

"The grill. Who's going to do the grilling?"

Shifting on the bed, Myles straddled Zabrina, his face inches from hers. He couldn't believe they'd spent ten years apart, shared a child, when they could've been together as a family. If he hadn't hung up on her, if he'd demanded they meet in person, he knew he could've convinced her to tell him the truth.

"You grill inside and Adam and I will grill outside, because it's a man thing."

"Are riding mowers and snowblowers man machines?"

"Hell, yeah," he drawled. "Now, if you're ready to take that shower I'll show you that it's big enough for two people. I'll pick you up and if you loop your legs around my waist it'll work."

"You know right well what happens when I put my legs around your waist."

"And—so?"

Zabrina gave her fiancé a long, penetrating stare, wondering what was going on behind his impassive gaze. "You *want* another baby, don't you?"

He blinked. "Yes, I want a child, but I also want time to get to know my son."

"How long do you want to wait after we're married to begin trying?"

"No more than six months, Brina."

"Okay, darling. You'll have your six months, but if I get the baby blues, then it may be sooner."

"What-eva," he drawled, laughing softly.

Zabrina was sitting on the porch when her aunt's hybrid car maneuvered into the driveway. She stood up, waiting for her son to get out, not wanting to react like overly excited mothers who rushed to their children coming home from camp or vacation. A smile softened her mouth when she saw him. His face was several shades darker, his curly hair was too long and he looked as if he'd grown at least half an inch. He saw her and bounded up the porch steps.

"Hey, Mom. I missed you."

Zabrina hugged him, burying her face in his hair. He seemed so much more mature. Her son was growing up. Pulling back, she examined his face. There was no doubt he was her child, but she also saw traces of Myles that she hadn't realized were there before. Adam had inherited her hair, her coloring and her eyes. But the expressive eyebrows and mouth were Myles's.

"I've missed you, too, Adam. You look wonderful. There must be something in the water in Virginia, because you've really grown."

The solid slam of the car door caught her attention. It wasn't her aunt who had brought Adam home, but her cousin. "Hey, Tanya. I thought Aunt Holly was bringing Adam home." Zabrina came off the porch and hugged her flight-attendant cousin, who changed her hairstyle every year. She'd cut her hair and styled it into twists. It was perfect for her small, round brown face.

"She had a migraine this morning, so I volunteered to bring him back."

"Why didn't you call me, Tanya? I would've driven down to get him."

"No biggie, Zee. I'd love to hang out with you, but I must get back. I have an early flight tomorrow morning. Let me get his bags out of the trunk, then I'm on my way."

"Don't you want to stay a couple of minutes and have something to drink?"

"Thanks, but I have everything I need in the car. Mom washed all of Adam's clothes, so he didn't bring back any laundry."

"Tell your mother to call when she feels better."

"I will." Tanya opened the trunk, removing a duffel and backpack. She kissed Zabrina and hugged Adam, then she was gone. It took her less than ten minutes before she was back on the road.

Zabrina stood with her arm around her son's shoulders,

waving until the hybrid's taillights disappeared. "How does it feel to be home?"

Adam smiled. "Good. I finished a lot of drawings. Do you want to see them?"

"Of course I do, but I need to talk to you."

Adam rolled his eyes. "Is it about going back to see Dr. Gordon?"

"No. Why?"

"I don't want to go back to counseling, Mom. I hate having to talk about Grandpa and my father."

"Are you sure, Adam?"

"I'm very sure, Mom."

"Promise me you'll let me know when you're feeling sad again."

"Aw, Mom!"

"Promise me, Adam."

He closed his eyes, his narrow chest rising and falling under a T-shirt with an image of President Barack Obama. "Okay, I promise. What do you want to talk about?"

"We'll talk inside." Picking up the duffel and leaving Adam to take the backpack, Zabrina led the way into the house and locked the door.

Zabrina sat across the table from Adam in the kitchen's breakfast nook, searching his face for a reaction to what she'd told him. She told him about Myles, how she'd fallen in love with him a long time ago, that they'd planned to marry before she married Thomas Cooper and that they'd found each other again, and this time they would marry and become a family.

"When are you getting married, Mom?"

Her chin trembled noticeably. Her son's voice was a

monotone. It was obvious he wasn't happy that she had a man in her life. "We haven't set a date."

"Why?"

"We're buying a house." She made certain to say *we* rather than *I* or *Myles*. Zabrina had to impress upon her son that they were to be a family unit.

"Where?"

"It's near Pittsburgh."

"Why do we have to move there? What's wrong with Philadelphia?"

"There's nothing wrong with Philadelphia. Myles works in Pittsburgh. He teaches at a law school."

"He's a lawyer?"

"Yes, Adam. He's a lawyer."

Adam chewed his lip. "When am I going to meet him?"

"When would you like to meet him?"

"Now."

"Okay."

Zabrina got up and went over to the wall phone. It took less than a minute to relay Adam's request. She walked out of the house to wait on the porch. It was about to begin. It'd taken a decade for a father-and-son reunion.

Myles felt his heart stop then start up again when he saw his son for the first time. Adam looked like Zabrina, but there were subtle similarities that indicated the boy was his. The most startling resemblance was the hands. All of the Eaton men had the same hands. The first joint on the right pinky was a little crooked.

He held out his right hand. "Hello, Adam. I'm Myles."

Adam stared at the proffered hand, then shook it. "Hello."

Myles knew he had to take the initiative or they would

continue to stare at each other. "There's a hammock in the back where we can talk." It was as close as he could get to his flesh and blood without making him feel uncomfortable.

Adam nodded. "Okay."

Myles led his son around to the back of the house. He heard the soft gasp from Adam when he saw the hammock. He showed him the technique for getting in, then stood back to allow him to execute it. The young boy got in on the first try, Myles followed, lying at the opposite end.

They swung back and forth for a full five minutes before Adam asked, "Are you nice to my mom?"

The question was not one Myles would've predicted from the boy. "Yes, I am, Adam. I'm very, very nice to your mother."

"Mr. Cooper wasn't nice to her."

"You called him Mr. Cooper?"

"That's what he wanted me to call him because everyone called him that."

Myles wished that Thomas Cooper were still alive so he could beat the hell out of him. "I'm nice to your mother because I love her. I've loved her for a very long time."

"Mom told me that you're going to get married."

"That's true, Adam."

"Will that make me your son?"

Struggling not to break down in front of his son, Myles took a deep breath. "Yes. It will make you my son. And if you want, your mother and I can change your name so you will be Adam Eaton instead of Adam Cooper."

Adam sat up. "Can you do that?"

"Yes, I can."

"When?"

"After your mother and I marry."

"Can you marry now?"

Myles also sat up. He'd thought Adam would resent him marrying his mother. "I guess we can. But I have to ask your mother if that's what she wants."

"She said she wants to marry you."

"I know that, and I want to marry her."

"But why can't you do it now?"

Myles didn't want to be manipulated by a ten-year-old even if he was his son. He gave him a level stare. "Your mother and I will talk about it. Okay?"

Adam nodded. "Okay."

"What do you like to do?"

"Draw."

"What do you draw?" Myles asked.

"Comics."

"Do you want to show me your drawings?"

"My mom doesn't like me to draw because she says she wants me to grow up to be a doctor or a lawyer."

You can grow up to be anything you want to be. Myles knew he was in for a fight with Zabrina, but he wanted their son to choose his own path. His father had wanted him to become a doctor, and he'd chosen law. If Adam wanted to be an artist, then, as his father, he would try to make it happen.

"Go get your drawings, Adam."

He waited in the hammock while the lanky kid with the mop of curly hair ran into the house. He returned with a sketch pad and a tin filled with colored pencils. Reaching over, Myles pulled Adam into the hammock and sat, stunned, as he stared at the colored images filling up the pages.

Adam was more than a good artist. He was exceptional. In fact, he was better than Myles had been at his age. "I used to draw, too."

"You did?"

"Yes," Myles said proudly. "But I never showed my work to anyone."

Excitement fired the gold in Adam's eyes. "What did you draw?"

"I liked drawing the Justice League of America."

"I draw the JLA, too," Adam said excitedly. The fictional DC Comics superhero team was a favorite of his. Turning the pad to a clean page, he handed Myles a pencil. "Who's your favorite in the team?"

Supporting the pad on his knees, Myles began making light strokes on the blank sheet of paper. "I like Black Canary and Flash."

Scooting over until he was seated next to Myles, Adam stared at the strokes taking shape. "I like Green Lantern, Batman and Captain Marvel. That's so cool. You're drawing Flash."

"It may be cool, but your drawings are much better. What grade are you in?"

Adam leaned closer, resting his head on Myles's shoulder to get a better view of the sketch. "I'm going into the seventh grade."

Myles stopped sketching and gave him a sidelong glance. "Do you mean the sixth grade?"

"It's the seventh. I went from the third grade to the fifth because fourth-grade work was too easy for me."

Hot damn! Not only was his son talented, but he was gifted. Myles lost track of time as he and Adam sketched the characters of the JLA. The sun had shifted lower in the summer sky when Zabrina came out of the house.

"Look, Mom! Myles and I are drawing together."

Moving closer to the hammock, she stared, stunned at

the many characters on the sketch pad. She recognized Batman, Superman and Wonder Woman. "I didn't know you could draw," she said to Myles.

"That's because I was a closet sketcher. Adam's drawings are phenomenal."

"I know he's good."

Leaning over, Adam smiled at his mother. "Can I take lessons, Mom? Please."

"I'll have to think about it."

"What's there to think about, Brina?" Myles asked. "The kid is exceptional."

"Yeah, Mom. I'm exceptional. And Myles said he was going to take me to Pittsburgh tomorrow to see our new house. Do you want to come?"

Zabrina couldn't believe how quickly father and son had bonded. "I don't think so, darling. I have a few things I have to do around the house. You and Myles can go without me."

She would give father and son their time alone to get to know each other better. After all, she'd had her son for ten years and now it was time for her to share him with his father. Myles had come into Adam's life at the right time, because a boy approaching manhood needed a positive male role model in his life.

Adam was in bed when Myles and Zabrina crawled into the hammock together. They lay together without talking. It was a time when words weren't necessary.

It was Myles who broke the silence. "Adam asked why we couldn't get married now."

Zabrina's body stiffened before relaxing. "Why?"

She listened as Myles repeated what their son had said about Thomas Cooper. Her eyes filled with tears and rolled down her face when she realized what she'd done to her son by staying married to Thomas. It was apparent the child had seen and heard things she'd sought to shield from him.

"What have I done to my baby, Myles? I thought I was protecting him—"

"Stop it, Brina. You can't beat up on yourself for something over which you had no control. You did what you thought was best for yourself and your father."

"But I almost ruined our son."

"You didn't ruin him. Living with someone like Cooper taught him how *not* to treat a woman. Our son needs a normal life with a mother and father who love him and one another. What do you say, baby girl? Do I make an honest woman out of you, or are you going to turn into a low-class ho?"

"I'll low-class ho you, Myles Adam Eaton, when I make you go cold turkey."

"If you do that then we can't give Adam a brother or sister."

The seconds ticked. "You're right."

"I can make it happen in a couple of days."

"How?" Zabrina asked.

"We can apply for a license and I'll ask Judge Stacey Greer-Monroe to marry us."

"Where do you want to hold the ceremony?"

"I'll ask Belinda and Griffin if we can use their place. If the weather holds, then we can have it outdoors."

"When are we going to do this, Myles?"

"Next Saturday."

Zabrina closed her eyes. She didn't want to wait too long because she didn't want anything to come up that would prevent her from becoming Mrs. Myles Eaton. "Call Belinda."

Chapter 16

"Who wants more?" Zabrina lifted the corner of the French toast with the spatula, testing it for doneness before flipping it over on the stovetop grill.

"I do," Myles answered.

"Me, too." Adam garbled. His mouth was filled with food.

"Don't talk with food in your mouth," Myles and Zabrina said in unison.

"Okay," he mumbled.

Zabrina glared at her son. "Adam, you're still talking with food in your mouth."

"Sorry," he apologized after swallowing. "Can I have another sausage, too, Mom?"

"How many does that make?"

"I only had two. And, they were small."

Zabrina didn't want to call attention to Adam's sudden increase in appetite, because for years he'd been a picky eater. Spending a month with his cousins had definitely changed his attitude when it came to eating. Tanya's eleven- and thirteen-year-old sons were programmed to eat any and everything on their plates, including vegetables, or forfeit television and video-game privileges.

She'd gotten up early to prepare breakfast for Myles and Adam before they set out for Pittsburgh. Myles had promised to show the boy the house and have a late lunch at his favorite Steel City restaurant before driving back to Philly where they would go out for dinner as a family unit for the first time.

"What about you, Myles? Do you want more sausage?"

Myles shook his head. "No thanks. I'm good here."

He glanced at his watch. It was close to seven-thirty and he wanted to be on the road by eight. With a little more than three hundred miles between Philly and Pittsburgh he hoped to reach his destination before one. Usually when he drove alone he tended to speed, but with Adam in the car he knew he would have to keep to the speed limit.

The doorbell rang and everyone went completely still. "Are you expecting anyone?" he asked Zabrina.

She lifted her shoulder. "It's probably Rachel." It wasn't often Zabrina had early morning visitors. The exception was her neighbor.

Rachel's children were home after an extended stay with their grandparents, who'd indulged their every whim. It'd taken Rachel two weeks to get them back on a mealtime and bedtime schedule. She'd always had problems getting Shane and Maggie up in the morning so they would catch their respective school buses. Maggie and Shane's return had curtailed their mother's social life because her first date with Hugh had escalated to a minimum of two times a week.

Myles stood up. "I'll get the door."

Taking long strides, he walked out of the kitchen. He reached the door and peered through a sidelight. It wasn't Rachel. Opening the door, he nodded to a diminutive man. His eyes, in a dark weathered face, were smiling and he looked as if he'd slept in his seersucker suit.

"Good morning. May I help you?"

"Does Zabrina Cooper live here?"

"Who's asking?"

The man straightened as if the gesture would add an additional inch or two to his slight frame. "My name is Russell Newton. I am…was Isaac Mixon's attorney. I'm retiring and my secretary was packing up my files when she found this." Reaching into the inside of his rumpled jacket, he pulled out a white envelope. "Unfortunately, it was misfiled. It should've been delivered to Mr. Mixon's daughter within six months of his passing." He smiled, displaying a set of yellowing teeth. "But I always say, better late than never."

Myles extended his hand. "I'm Ms. Mixon's fiancé. I'll give it to her."

"No, no, no. I was instructed to give it to her personally."

He wanted to tell the man that he was more than six months too late. Isaac Mixon had died in his sleep last June, and pursuant to his instructions it should've been delivered to Zabrina on or before December. It was now early August, eight months later than the deadline.

"Who is it, Myles?"

He turned at Zabrina's approach. "Mr. Newton is here to give you something." Resting a hand at the small of her back, he dropped a kiss on her hair and then left her to deal with the odd little man.

"Would you like to come in, Mr. Newton?"

"No, no, no. I can't stay. My granddaughter is waiting in the car for me. I just came to give you this." He handed her the envelope. "It's from your father."

Zabrina's eyelids fluttered wildly. "What do you mean it's from my father? Isaac Mixon died almost a year ago."

Russell Newton ran a gnarled hand over a pate with sparse patches of white hair. "Mr. Mixon came to me and asked me to help him draw up a statement. It's not a last will and testament but more like a final confession. I witnessed it and so did my secretary."

"Why did you wait this long to give it to me?"

"I told your fiancé that it was misfiled. I just retired and I'm transferring my client files to another attorney. I know your father wanted you to see this, so I decided to deliver it personally."

Zabrina managed a tight smile. "Thank you, Mr. Newton."

He gave her a shaky bow. "You're welcome, Mrs. Cooper."

She watched the elderly man as he carefully navigated the porch steps and shuffled to the car parked behind Myles's Range Rover. Waiting until the driver backed out of the driveway and maneuvered down the street, she sat on the rocker and opened the sealed envelope. There was a single sheet of paper with a small key taped to the back.

Her eyes scanned the type, her eyes filling and making it impossible to see the words. Pressing a fist to her mouth, she bit down hard to keep from screaming. She didn't believe it. She couldn't believe it. She'd married and spent a decade with a depraved monster all for nothing.

Zabrina was still sitting on the rocker, her fist against her mouth when Myles returned to the porch. He saw the letter and hunkered down next to her. "What's the matter, baby?"

She shoved the paper at him. "Read it, Myles. Aloud, so I can hear what I've just read, because I still don't believe it."

Sitting on the footstool, Myles cleared his throat. "'My dearest daughter. I've instructed Russell Newton to deliver this to you—call it my confession—within six months of my passing. I am sorry you had to sacrifice the love of your life because of me—all because I was too much of a coward to stand up to Thomas Cooper and his hired muscle.

"'Thomas set me up to take a fall because of what I saw. I walked in on him taking a bribe from John Gallagher, a small-time hood the Philadelphia Police Department and the feds have on their organized crime radar. I left, thinking it was over, but a week later I got a visit from a stranger with a message from Gallagher's boss: *Forget what you saw or your daughter will find herself placing flowers on her father's grave.* Thomas came to see me later that evening, talking about how he needed to improve his image with a wife before he officially announced he was a candidate for mayor. That's when he mentioned your name. When I told him that you were engaged to marry Myles Eaton, he said that was of no consequence to him.

"'The sonofabitch concocted the story about me stealing from him, and then him having to pay off my gambling debts so I wouldn't inform on him. I've never bet on anything in my life. I've never even bought a lottery ticket. I hate that you had to become a pawn in something so heinous and depraved and that my grandson was deprived of the love and protection of his biological father.

"'And if you ever had a question as to whether Emory Davidson would've shot me, then the answer is yes. Would he have killed me? No. But I doubt whether I would've been able to walk again. His trademark is leaving his victims crippled or permanently maimed. I wasn't afraid for myself, precious daughter. I was afraid for you and the child you were carrying.

"'I've also told you that I believe in payback and you know what they say about payback: it's a bitch. The key taped on the reverse side opens the jewelry box that belonged to your mother. I took photos of Thomas's clandestine meetings that will shock a lot of people who've made Senator Thomas Cooper a demigod. Take the photos and this letter to the DA. I wish I could be there to see Thomas Cooper's fall from grace, but if he goes before me, you'll be free. And, if he goes after me, you still will be free to live your life as you should have. I have one other request: please let Myles Eaton know that Adam is his son. Love always, Dad.'"

Arms wrapped around her middle, Zabrina rocked back and forth as if in a catatonic state. She hadn't read wrong. Her father had sacrificed himself not to save his life, but to save hers. Hers and Adam's.

"Myles is my real father."

Adam had come out onto the porch without making a sound. Zabrina stopped rocking and Myles stood, meeting the wide-eyed gaze of the boy who'd probably overheard what he'd read aloud.

"Are you really my dad?" The last word was a sob.

Myles nodded, because his constricted throat wouldn't allow him to speak. The seconds ticked until he finally found the ability to speak the words. "Yes, Adam, I am your dad."

Adam took a step, his gaze shifting from his father to his mother. "When did you find out you were my father?"

Resisting the urge to reach out and cradle his son to

his chest, to tell him he would protect him as he'd promised to protect his mother, he said, "Your mother told me two days ago."

"Why didn't she tell you before? That way you could've come and got me from Mr. Cooper."

Myles pushed his hands into the back pockets of his jeans. He wanted to comfort his son, reassure him the horror he'd experienced was over and would never be repeated. "If I'd known, Adam, I would've come to get you *and* your mother. No one or anything could've stopped me."

Adam pointed at Zabrina. "It's her fault."

"No, it's not her fault."

"Yes, it is. She should've called you."

Myles took a step and grasped his son's hand. "Come into the house with me."

Zabrina shot up as if impaled by a sharp object. "No, Myles!"

He gave her a chilling stare. Did she actually believe he would harm the boy? He hadn't had to play daddy but knew he would be much better in the role than Thomas Cooper. "Stay out of this, Brina. My son and I have to talk."

The tension seemed to leave Zabrina as she sank back to the rocker. She blew out a breath. She had to trust Myles and she had to prepare herself to share her son with him. "I'll be here," she said in resignation.

Myles winked at her as he opened the door and let Adam precede him into the house and back to the kitchen. Sitting at the breakfast nook, he sat opposite the boy who looked as if he were close to tears.

"Adam, son, you can't blame your mother over something she couldn't control. She married and stayed with Thomas Cooper not only to protect you but also your grandfather."

Adam's chin trembled. "But…but why didn't she call you?"

"Even if she'd called me I probably wouldn't have taken her call. I was very, very angry with your mother at that time."

"Are you angry now?"

"No, Adam. I'm not angry now."

"Do you love my mom?"

An expression of tenderness softened Myles's masculine features. "Yes, I do. I've always loved your mother. Even when I was angry with her I still loved her."

"Why did she lie, Dad?"

Dad rolled off the child's tongue as if he'd acknowledged Myles as his father for years instead of minutes. "She didn't lie, son. Your mother couldn't say anything because she believed your grandfather would've been arrested and sent to prison."

"Grandpa wasn't bad."

Myles smiled. "No, he wasn't. Your grandfather was one of the best men I've ever known."

Adam's expressive eyebrows lifted. "You knew Grandpa?"

"Yes. I knew your mother when she was just a little girl. She and my sister Belinda became best friends. Speaking of my sister, I want you to know that you have a couple of aunts, an uncle and twin cousins whom I'm certain will be glad to meet you. And then there are my parents, who are your grandparents. I'm going to have to warn you in advance that your Gram is going to act a little silly when she discovers she has a grandson."

"Does she have another grandson?"

"No. She only has granddaughters."

"When am I going to meet them?"

Adam's query gave Myles pause. He'd e-mailed the Realtor, telling her he wanted to see the house that afternoon, and she'd juggled her busy schedule to accommodate him. "Most likely it'll be tomorrow, because we have to go to Pittsburgh today."

A hint of a smile played at the corners of Adam's mouth. "When am I going to meet my cousins?"

"I'll call their aunt and uncle once we get on the road."

"When are you and Mom getting married?"

"Why?"

Adam's eyebrows nearly met when he frowned. "I don't want the kids in school to call her names."

Myles, leaning over the table, gave his son a withering stare. "I don't ever want to hear you call your mother a bad name. In fact I don't want you to call any female a bad name. Do you understand me?"

"Yes, Myles—I mean, Dad. But all the boys at my school do."

"I don't care what they say. No son of mine will ever disrespect a woman." He put out his fist, smiling when Adam touched it with his. "To answer your question as to when your mother and I are getting married, I still don't know. I called a friend who is a judge, but I have to wait for her to call me back. Right now I'm living in my sister's house not far from here. I'm going to ask your mother if you can spend a few nights with me so we can do guy things."

Adam's eyes narrowed. "What guy things, Dad?"

Myles lifted his shoulders. "I don't know. We'll think of something."

"What about a burping contest?" Adam suggested. "I can burp real loud. But, don't tell Mom because she gets real mad when I do it."

"It'll be our secret," Myles whispered. He laughed when Adam put out his fist for another bump. "Do you like dogs?" he asked his son as they walked out of the kitchen to return to the porch.

"I love them. I wanted one, but Mr. Cooper was allergic to dogs."

"When we move to Pittsburgh I'll let you pick out the one you want. Your cousins Sabrina and Layla each have a Yorkshire terrier."

"Those are girl dogs, Dad. Boys have big dogs."

Dropping an arm over his son's shoulders, Myles pulled him close. "That's *my* boy."

Zabrina's long wait to become Mrs. Myles Eaton was going to end within minutes. Dr. Dwight Eaton led her over the red carpet at the rear of Griffin and Belinda Rice's house to where Myles stood with their son as his best man. She'd chosen a simple silk slip-dress gown with a seed-pearl bodice and a hem that flowed into a train. In lieu of a veil she wore a small pillbox hat covered with pearls.

Judge Stacey Greer-Monroe, in a black robe, stood ready to begin the ceremony that would bind Myles and Zabrina together as husband and wife. She'd been vacationing at her Puerto Rico condo when Myles had called to ask her to officiate at his wedding. Leaving her daughter with her husband, she'd booked a flight back to do the honor.

She was just as surprised as most Philadelphians when the news of the late Senator Thomas Cooper's association with known and suspected criminals appeared in the headlines. She was grateful that Myles was moving his wife and son across the state to live in Pittsburgh where they wouldn't be hounded by reporters and photographers.

Stacey smiled at Dr. Dwight Eaton when he placed Zabrina's hand in Myles's outstretched one. She wanted to tell Zabrina that she was one of the luckiest women in the City of Brotherly Love, having captured the heart of a man destined to one day sit on the bench. What she hadn't told Myles was that there was talk of appointing him to replace one of several judges who were rumored to be retiring in the very near future.

Zabrina smiled at Belinda, who was her matron of honor. It had been a long time coming, but both had managed to marry the men they'd loved for more years than they could remember.

Zabrina's Aunt Holly, Tanya and her husband and sons had driven from Falls Church the night before to meet the Eatons during the rehearsal dinner. Rachel and her children were warmly greeted by the Eatons. Myles's college and law-school friends came despite the short notice, and Hugh Ormond had volunteered to prepare the food for the reception.

She and Myles would enjoy a four-day honeymoon in Bermuda before returning to Philadelphia. They had another two weeks before they would close on the house, and the following week the fall semester at Duquesne was scheduled to begin.

Their original plan—for her and Adam to remain in Philly until renovations to the house were completed—was scrapped, because Adam complained that he didn't want to be separated from his father. Zabrina suspected the tree house, the promise of a dog and the hours he spent drawing with Myles were the catalyst for an almost instantaneous bond between father and son. They would live in one section of the house during the renovations and Adam would be enrolled in a private school less than a mile away.

She smiled at Myles when he gave her fingers a gentle squeeze. Her voice was clear, carrying easily in the garden as she repeated her vows. "I take thee, Myles Adam Eaton, to be my lawful wedded husband, to have and to hold from this day forward." She slipped a wide platinum band on his left hand.

Myles's baritone echoed as he repeated his vows, slipping a matching band on Zabrina's finger. A shaft of sunlight reflected off the stones in her engagement ring.

Judge Monroe winked at Myles. "By the power vested in me by the Commonwealth of Pennsylvania, I now pronounce you husband and wife. Myles, you may kiss your bride."

Wrapping his arms around Zabrina's waist, he lifted her off her feet and devoured her mouth as the assembled family and friends applauded and whistled. Passion and love were definitely sweeter and sexier the second time around.

REQUEST YOUR FREE BOOKS!

2 FREE NOVELS
PLUS 2 *FREE GIFTS!*

KIMANI
ROMANCE™

Love's ultimate destination!

KROM09

HELP CELEBRATE
ARABESQUE'S
15TH ANNIVERSARY!

ARABESQUE®

2009 marks Arabesque's 15th anniversary!

Help us celebrate by telling us about your most special memories and moments with Arabesque books. Entries will be judged by the Arabesque Anniversary Committee based on which are the most touching and well written. Fifteen lucky winners will receive as a prize a full-grain leather duffel bag with the Arabesque anniversary logo.

VISIT **WWW.MYSPACE.COM/KIMANIPRESS**
FOR THE COMPLETE OFFICIAL RULES